"It looks as if we're stuck with each other—at least for the next little while."

"Stuck with each other? Oh, I don't think so!" said Emily.

"You have some other solution up your sleeve?"

"Well I...Lucas, I couldn't possibly stay another night under the same roof as you!"

"Why not?" he drawled. "Forewarned is forearmed. I have a lock on my bedroom door and I'll make a point of using it."

CATHERINE SPENCER, once an English teacher, fell into writing through eavesdropping on a conversation about Harlequin romances. Within two months she changed careers, and sold her first book to Harlequin in 1984. She moved to Canada from England thirty years ago and lives in Vancouver. She is married to a Canadian and has four grown children—two daughters and two sons—plus three dogs and a cat. In her spare time she plays the piano, collects antiques and grows tropical shrubs.

CATHERINE SPENCER

Tempting Lucas

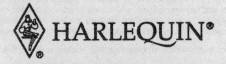

HARLEQUIN®

TORONTO • NEW YORK • LONDON
AMSTERDAM • PARIS • SYDNEY • HAMBURG
STOCKHOLM • ATHENS • TOKYO • MILAN • MADRID
PRAGUE • WARSAW • BUDAPEST • AUCKLAND

ISBN 0-373-11976-3

TEMPTING LUCAS

First North American Publication 1998.

This edition published by arrangement with Harlequin Books S.A.

® and TM are trademarks of the publisher. Trademarks indicated with ® are registered in the United States Patent and Trademark Office, the Canadian Trade Marks Office and in other countries.

Printed in U.S.A.

CHAPTER ONE

SHE hadn't been back to Belvoir in eleven years, not since the year that she'd lost the baby. At the very least the place could have looked as if it had missed her a fraction as much as she'd missed it—shown its age a little, the way she was sure she showed hers. But no. It rose out of the morning mist, as pale and beautiful today as it had been then, evoking not just the innocent pleasures of her childhood but the sharp unhappiness of unrequited love and lost dreams as well.

Wisteria still wound in mauve clusters around the pillars supporting the upper balconies, the way it had every spring since her grandmother had come there as a bride. Gauzy white curtains still swirled over the windows of the corner turrets, and the brass bell at the massive front entrance gleamed with the same golden brilliance.

How often, when they'd been children, had they rung that bell for the sheer mischief of it, and brought one or other of the servants running and scolding? But not today.

"Miss Emily!" Consuela, who'd served as general factotum at Belvoir since before Emily had been born, bared her yellow old teeth in a smile. "What a welcome sight you are! *Madame* will be so pleased to see you."

"Humph!" her grandmother grumbled, scowling over the half-glasses perched on her patrician nose when Emily stepped into the morning room. "I suppose I should be grateful that they had the good grace to send you to badger me, Emily Jane. Of them all, you at least have the wit to keep me entertained. You may kiss me, child."

Emily bent, touched her lips to the papery cheek, and clamped down viciously on the tears suddenly damming behind her eyes. "You're looking well, Grand-mère."

"And you lie graciously but badly," Monique Lamartine said. "Having you here might prove even more diverting than I'd anticipated, provided you understand that I am not about to move out of my house no matter what sort of pressure you bring to bear on me. I lived here with your grandfather and I intend to lie beside him in my grave, though not quite as quickly as my son and daughters might like. The body is a little frailer but the mind..." She tapped her forehead. "It's still sound, never doubt that, and I will continue to lead my life as *I* see fit. So you're very welcome to visit for a while, Emily Jane, but when you decide to leave you will not be taking me with you."

Emily murmured something innocuous and tried again to hide her dismay. Monique Lamartine rose in her memory tall and proud and invincible; this shrunken, enfeebled old lady with the stick propped next to her chair bore little resemblance to the woman she knew as Grandmother.

Consuela reappeared, wheeling before her a trolley laden with sterling and translucent Limoges china. A tiered silver cake stand of delicacies baked fresh that morning occupied pride of place on the lower shelf.

"Pour the tea, Emily Jane, and give yourself something to do until you've composed yourself," Monique ordered tartly.

In all the years Emily had known her, her grandmother had preferred coffee, a rich, full-bodied French roast in keeping with her ancestry. "I didn't know you drank tea, Grand-mère."

"There are a lot of things you don't know," her grandmother retorted. "That tends to happen when you avoid a person for over ten years."

Emily was thirty and long past the age, or so she'd thought, when anyone could make her flush and feel as awkward as a teenager. But her grandmother's barbed observation found its mark. The telltale pink spread over her face despite her attempt to rationalize what she knew must seem like inexcusable neglect on her part.

"I haven't avoided you! You were at my wedding, and we saw each other again at Suzanne's, a few months after. We celebrated New Year's together in San Francisco four years ago, and met at the family reunion in Charleston when Peter graduated from the academy. We've talked on the phone, I've written, and sent you postcards whenever I've gone traveling."

The rest of her might have dwindled, but Monique's scorn had lost none of its sting. "I don't know how long it took you to memorize such an impressive list, Emily Jane, but let me assure you it was a waste of time. On all those occasions, we were surrounded by other relatives and, of necessity, confined to meaningless exchanges which neither one of us particularly enjoyed. Of course, there was, as there always has been, another option, one which would have allowed us the privacy to reinforce those ties formed when you were a girl, but you chose not to employ it. You have not set foot in my home since the summer you turned nineteen."

Emily looked away as a different sort of shame overwhelmed her. "It wasn't you I was avoiding, Grand-mère, it was this house, this place. I wouldn't be here now—"

"If it weren't for the fact that my children think I'm incapable of looking after myself, so they've bribed you to try to get me to see things their way because they know that, for all that you've neglected me so abysmally for far too long, you're still my favorite. Well, it doesn't say much for you, Emily Jane, does it, that I had to be half crippled by a stroke before you could bring yourself to put aside your own feelings and give a thought to mine?''

"I'm sorry, Grand-mère."

Emily didn't for a moment expect that such an answer would be found acceptable, which was why she almost missed the cup into which she was pouring fragrant Lapsang Souchong tea when her grandmother said quite gently, "I know you are, child, and I know why you found coming back here so painful. It was that Flynn boy from next door."

"I'm not sure I understand what you mean, Grand-mère."

Monique's sympathy vanished in a flash. "Give me credit for having some intelligence, for pity's sake! I saw the way you languished, the last summer you spent here, dreaming the hours away in the belvedere, hoping he'd show up, coming alive only when he deigned to spare you a moment's attention."

"Puppy love," Emily said, regaining enough poise to pass a cup of tea to her grandmother without spilling a drop in the saucer. "All girls go through it."

"Not all girls sneak out of the house after dark and return long after other respectable souls are asleep in their beds. Not all girls shut themselves away from the people around them, preferring to spend their time in seclusion, nor do they mark off the days in their diaries with quite the assiduous care with which you marked off yours, the last few weeks of that summer."

"You read my diary?" Appalled, Emily stared at her grandmother.

"Certainly I read your diary," Monique said, with shameless relish. "How else was I supposed to discover what was troubling you so deeply? You allowed that...that *rogue* to rob you of your innocence, and then you worried yourself into a near breakdown wondering if you'd been left with child.''

"Left with child". Such an old-fashioned, genteel way to characterize the disgrace an illegitimate pregnancy would have brought to the family. Given that that was exactly the predicament in which Emily had found herself, how was it that ultimately being left *without* child had such a destitute ring to it?

"Fortunately you were spared that," Monique went on, blithely ignorant of the aftermath of that summer, "though even had you not been it would not have changed my love for you. You were always my special child."

Emily's eyes burned again with unshed tears. "Oh, Grand-mère!"

"I saw your face the day he came lollygagging over here and announced his engagement to that woman. Had your grandfather been alive, he'd have horse-whipped him. As it is, Lucas Flynn got his just deserts when not all his fancy medical training could save his wife and he had to bury her in· some heathen African country. The pity of it is that whatever killed her didn't carry him off too. The world does not need men like him."

"I understand he's a very fine doctor."

Her grandmother let out the closest to a snort that she'd ever permit herself. "Not any more he isn't! His doctoring days are over. Seems he lost his taste for medicine, or else his nerve. These days he's a recluse, emerging into view only when conscience drives him to earn his keep around the house as a general handyman."

In the short time since she'd arrived at Belvoir, Emily had weathered a range of emotions. She'd experienced nostalgia, shame, sadness and shock. To that list she now added dread. "What house? The last I heard, Lucas Flynn was running a clinic somewhere in Central Africa."

"Then your information is sadly out of date," Monique declared flatly. "Lucas Flynn is living next door with his grandmother. The neighborhood, I fear, has gone to the dogs since you were last here, Emily Jane.''

Her worst nightmare—having to face him again—had come to pass! Practically stammering with dismay, Emily asked, ''But how—*why* is he here?''

''Because he's a failure! What possible other reason could he have for letting his medical license lapse? And why else would his benighted grandmother feel compelled to make excuses for him every time she opens her mouth?''

''Excuses?'' Emily repeated faintly. ''Lucas Flynn was never the type to hide behind excuses, Grand-mère.''

''He is now,'' Monique said with a satisfied little nod. ''Spends half his time shut up in some university lab, peering into a microscope, and the other half recording his findings—except, as I just mentioned, when he deigns to mow the lawn or otherwise make himself useful next door. A bit of a come-down, wouldn't you say, compared to his former grandiose laying-on-of-healing-hands plans?''

''There isn't a university in April Water,'' Emily said, still groping for the magic key that would release her from a dream that threatened to become worse long before it grew any better. Wasn't confronting the shocking reality of her grandmother's declining health enough, without this added complication?

''There are plenty in the San Francisco area,'' Monique replied, then spoilt the possibility of reprieve by adding, ''Not that he spends every waking hour there, what with all the fancy computer equipment he's rumored to have had installed at Roscommon House. But why are we wasting breath on a man like him when we have more important matters to discuss, such as your marriage?''

She took Emily's ringless left hand in hers. ''Don't make me drag the details out of you a syllable at a time, Emily Jane. I never expected it would last, of course, but that doesn't mean I'm not interested in knowing how it ended."

"We grew apart." Emily shrugged, at a loss to know how to explain the lack of passion that had characterized her relationship with George.

"You were never together. Ambition and career advancement lured him to the altar and penance drove you."

"That's not fair, Grand-mère. George tried hard to be the sort of husband he thought I wanted. We both tried, but if anyone's to blame for it all ending in divorce I am."

Monique's black eyes focused shrewdly on Emily's face. "Why? Because you were married to one man and pining for another?"

How could her grandmother have known? Emily wondered. Was it written all over her face, as plain to see as if she'd actually committed adultery? "If you're talking about the business with Lucas Flynn, Grand-mère—"

"Of course I am."

"That all ended three years before I got engaged." But the memory had remained vivid, embroidered to an unlikely magic by the passage of time. Had George sensed it? Was that what eventually had driven him into another woman's arms and bed?

"I'm leaving you, Emily," he'd announced over eggs Benedict, one rainy Sunday morning nearly eighteen months ago. "There's someone else."

"Do I know her?" Emily had asked, as politely as if they'd been discussing a fourth for bridge. Because, of course, Lucas had always been the third member of the party, even if his name never crossed her lips.

"No." George had nudged his coffee-cup closer for a refill. "Just as well, probably. Less awkward all round."

What had shocked Emily had not been that her marriage was coming to an abrupt and unexpected end, but that she had accepted the news with staggering equanimity. She'd added cream and two lumps of sugar to her husband's coffee and, in the sort of tone that she might have murmured, "Have another croissant, dear" said, "I suppose you'd like a divorce."

"Might as well. No immediate rush, of course, though I'd as soon not wait too long."

"Do you miss him, Emily Jane?"

Emily blinked and looked at her grandmother in confusion. "Who? George?"

"If you thought I meant Lucas Flynn, then it's small wonder your marriage failed. Even men like George Keller have their pride. Bad enough you were a melancholy bride, without compounding the sin and betraying yourself as a dissatisfied wife."

"Perhaps if there'd been children—"

"It's a blessing there weren't!"

"But if there had been we might have felt we shared something worth saving."

"In my day," her grandmother observed with caustic insight, "a husband and wife took it upon themselves to make their marriage work. They didn't expect innocent children to rescue it from its troubles."

"But I think the lack of children made George feel inadequate. I think he blamed himself."

"As he should. You come from select but hardy stock, Emily Jane. It's hardly likely you'd have been unable to produce an heir had the opportunity presented itself."

Was it? Emily had wondered many times since if the punishment for her short-lived, unhappy illegitimate pregnancy had been the absence of babies later on, when it would have been perfectly acceptable for her to bear them. "His new wife gave birth within six months of their getting married."

"The hussy!" Monique hissed on an outraged breath. "They deserve each other!"

"George is a perfectly nice man, Grand-mère. He just wasn't the right man for me."

Her grandmother eyed her narrowly. "No, he wasn't, any more than that rogue from next door was. Dare I hope, Emily Jane, that you've learned your lesson and will choose more judiciously in future?"

In light of her recent discoveries about Lucas, and their effect on her peace of mind, that was not a question Emily felt equal to answering honestly. However, she was spared having to lie because, when she glanced at her grandmother, she saw that, suddenly and quite completely, Monique had fallen asleep in her chair.

A fine wool shawl lay over the back of the sofa. Emily draped it carefully around her grandmother's frail shoulders, then stole from the room.

Consuela met her in the hall. "She's sleeping?"

Emily nodded. "Dropped off in a matter of seconds. Does that happen often?"

"More and more." Consuela sighed and looked as if she might say something else, then pressed her lips tightly together.

"What is it, Consuela?"

"Nothing—nothing. You see, don't you, that she's . . . ?"

"Old." The word emerged bathed in guilt and sadness. Why had she waited so long to come back when there was so little time left for Monique?

Consuela's hand on her arm was sympathetic. "It can't be helped, sweet child. Neither of us is getting any younger."

The truth of that became obvious over the next hour as Emily renewed her acquaintance with the house that held so many memories for her. Contrary to her first impression, the place was not as well kept as she'd thought. On the main floor, only the morning room, the small breakfast room and the kitchen were in daily use. The rest were closed off, their furnishings draped in dust sheets, and with cobwebs festooning the chandeliers. A light had burned out in the back hall and not been replaced, leaving the area dim even in the middle of the day.

"I'd have done it myself," Consuela said apologetically, when she caught Emily installing a fresh light bulb, "but I'm not so good with heights any more."

"Don't even *think* about using this stepladder," Emily scolded. "For heaven's sake, Consuela, why hasn't my grandmother brought in someone to give you extra help? It isn't as if she can't afford it."

"She is proud, just as she's always been. It grieves her to think we must call in strangers and let them see..." Consuela's voice trembled slightly "...that we cannot manage as we once did."

Emily could have wept anew with shame. "Come and talk to me while I prepare us all some lunch—and no, Consuela, don't try to talk me out of it! I'm perfectly capable in a kitchen and you've carried this burden long enough by yourself. It's past time my grandmother's family took some of the responsibility on themselves."

From the kitchen, she could see out to the sweep of lawn that once had been manicured to within an inch of its life. Now it ran unhindered into the untidy straggle of shrubbery lining the path to the river, reinforcing what was already apparent: the days were gone when Monique was mistress of all she surveyed. If she refused to leave Belvoir, someone would have to remain with her, to oversee the running of the estate as well as monitor her well-being. And there was little doubt who that someone would be.

Trying hard to be tactful, Emily brought up the subject that evening, during dinner. "Don't you miss being closer to the people you love, Grand-mère?"

"Not enough that I'm willing to move, just to be near them," Monique informed her.

"But if one of them was to live here at Belvoir, would you object?"

"That," her grandmother declared, "would depend entirely on which one of my so-called loved ones you have in mind, Emily Jane."

As if there'd ever been any question of the most suitable candidate! Who among the family had no personal ties elsewhere? Who, for that matter, was the only one who could get along with Monique for more than an hour at a time?

"I've been feeling that I need a change," she said, and it wasn't so far from the truth. "New England winters are long and cold, and Boston—"

"You have a business there. You told me once that you were very busy and very successful. Are you proposing to give it up, so that you can babysit a feeble old woman? Or is it my money you're after?"

"I neither want nor need your money, Grand-mère, but I do think I'd like to have your company. I didn't realize until this morning how much I've missed you."

"If you're asking if my door is open, Emily Jane, then let me remind you that it always has been. It was your choice to stay away, not mine."

Emily touched her serviette to her mouth. "Well, if it's all right with you, Grand-mère, I'd like to make up for lost time. May I come and live with you for a while?"

A tear splashed down Monique's wrinkled cheek and fell into her soup. "You may," she said, head lifted proudly to indicate that she wasn't about to acknowledge such a maudlin display of weakness.

Later, after the dishes were cleared away and Consuela had brought in the tea tray, Monique selected a cigarette from the silver box at her elbow and nodded to Emily to light it for her. "What about your business, Emily Jane? Will you sell it, or is there someone who can manage it for you during your absence?"

"I have a friend who's been interested in becoming a partner in Done To Perfection for about a year now. I think she'll be more than happy to buy me out."

"And you won't miss it?"

"If I do, I can always open up another branch here, once I'm settled. I like to be busy, Grand-mère. Come to that, I like being my own boss and making a success of things."

"Success is all very fine, child, but you can't warm your feet on it when you go to bed. Your grandfather has been dead seventeen years but I've never become used to sleeping alone. I miss him every night."

"Because you were happily married, that's why, but I'm not interested in that sort of life."

Choking a little as she inhaled, Monique peered through the smoke already wreathing her face. "It's unnatural for a woman your age to be so indifferent to men, Emily Jane, and it leads me to suspect you're hiding something. Is there, by chance, someone in your life that you don't want me to know about?"

"Certainly not," Emily said. But it was a lie. A new lie, scarcely more than a few hours old, to be sure, but a lie nonetheless. The back of her mind had been filled with his face, her heart with racing dread, ever since she'd learned that Lucas Flynn was widowed and living next door again.

Aware that her grandmother had fixed a very speculative gaze on her, Emily changed the subject. Pushing the ashtray a little closer to Monique's elbow, she asked, "Does your doctor know you smoke, Grand-mère?"

"Naturally. He's fool enough to think he has the right to know everything about me."

"And he doesn't object?"

"There's a difference between a fool and an imbecile, child. He knows better than to intrude with his opinions where they're not welcome."

"But it can't be good for you."

"If your reason for wanting to live here is that you plan to try to rearrange the way I choose to lead my life, Emily Jane, I shall withdraw my permission and you may leave first thing in the morning," Monique informed her acidly.

"I'm concerned for your health, that's all."

"When you reach my age, you'll realize that there's very little left that one can do for one's health except enjoy what remains of it. Which I intend to do by living where and with whom I please, and smoking when and where I feel like it." She puffed once or twice to underline her point and watched Emily through the veil of smoke curling up between them. "You look worn out, child. Don't feel you have to stay up entertaining me."

"I don't want to leave you down here by yourself."

"Why not? I'm used to it and I don't need sleep the way I once did. You have your old room in the southwest turret. Consuela spent most of the last week getting it ready for you."

Emily hid a yawn behind her hand. It had been a long day, made worse by the three hour time difference between Massachusetts and California. "If you're sure you don't mind, perhaps I will make an early night of it."

"Go," her grandmother ordered, rolling her eyes. "All this sudden attentive concern is beginning to annoy me."

The memories had besieged her from the moment she'd set foot in the house, but they saved their most potent attack until the end of the day when she was at her most vulnerable. Exhausted not only from travel but also from a succession of small shocks one on top of the other, Emily felt, when she opened her bedroom door, as if she'd stepped into a huge time tunnel running in reverse, and was helpless to stop it.

Everything conspired against her. Her clothes hung in one half of the vast armoire, her lingerie in the lined mahogany drawers of the other half, leaving her nothing with which to distract herself. Velvet-napped towels lay draped over the edge of the huge claw-footed tub in the attached bathroom. The covers were turned back on the bed, a Thermos of hot chocolate sat on the nightstand.

On the surface, nothing had changed. The delicate painted panelling, the carved four-poster with its embroidered tester, the cheval glass looked exactly as they always had, as though to say there was no rewriting history. But, most of all, the smells were what peeled back the years: gardenia bath essence and starched cotton sheets dried in the warm Californian sun; patchouli and the musty gentility of antique silk draperies. They overlapped her senses and sent her swimming back to that other time.

The curved windows in the turret wall stood open to the sweet night air, luring her deeper into the time tunnel. The sheen of moonlight illuminated the bend in the river beyond which she knew rose Roscommon House. When she had been nineteen and in love with Lucas Flynn, she had kept vigil at this window and known the second he had gone to his room because his light would shine through the night, and she, foolish romantic that she'd been, had thought of it as a beacon lighting a path from her heart to his.

She had been wrong.

If she had known he was here again, she would not have come back. But she had not known, and now it was too late.

She stepped closer to the windows to pull down the blinds. Involuntarily, her gaze stole to the right and with an accuracy undulled by time found the break in the trees which, during the day, revealed the steeply pitched roof of Roscommon and the gable which housed Lucas's room.

As if she'd activated a secret switch, a beam of light from his window suddenly pierced the darkness, as bright and golden as her hopes had been over eleven summers before.

She wanted to turn away. Even more, she wanted to stare at the sight and not care, not remember. But she was able to do neither. Remembrance flowed over her, merciless as a rogue wave sweeping its victim out to sea.

A breeze riffled past the gauzy white drapes and touched her skin. With a shudder, Emily pulled down the shades and shut out the sight of that light streaming through the darkness. Shut out the memories it brought with it.

She had been young then, barely out of school. Full of immature fantasies, no doubt, the way young women often were, but she'd grown up quickly, thanks to Lucas Flynn.

It didn't matter where he was living now. He could move into the room next door to hers for all she cared. Parade up and down in front of her, showing off his big, male body, and doing his best to reduce her to drooling lust. But he wouldn't succeed.

She'd never again give him the opportunity to flick her off as if she were just another summer insect buzzing around and annoying him. Nor would she allow him to spoil this special time with her beloved Grand-mère.

The mistakes had piled up, each more disastrous than its predecessor, that other summer. But she'd paid for them once, and dearly. She wasn't going to let him make her pay again.

He shut down the computer just after midnight, knowing it was futile trying to annotate scientific data from his latest experiments when his thoughts repeatedly strayed to events from much earlier times, before medicine had become his ruling passion.

As a doctor, he'd accepted long ago the human mind's amazing ability to connect telepathically with another, regardless of the time or distance separating them.

Sydney, thoroughly rooted in reality as she was, had scoffed at the idea, claiming it was the learned response that came of being a doctor, but he'd seen it as an instinct that couldn't be taught.

Either way, it all came down to the same thing now: when his grandmother had mentioned in passing that a member of Mrs. Lamartine's family had come to take care of her he'd known with absolute if unsubstantiated certainty that the visitor at Belvoir was Emily Jane. And once he'd allowed the knowledge to take hold there'd been no going back to his work.

Instead, he stood at the window of his room and stared out. It was one of those perfect nights midway between winter and spring—cool and still.

In the garden below, the magnolia tree had shed its petals, which lay like abandoned saucers on the grass. The scent of heliotrope filtered up, a sweet, heady perfume that he'd dreamed about when he was in Africa where the smell of death had permeated everything. Overhead, the sky was dappled with moonlight, a sprinkling of stars hung so low that he could almost have reached up and grasped a handful.

He had made the right decision in coming back here. It was home, and as different from Africa as heaven was from hell. It defined his boyhood, his youth, and his emergence as a man, and held none of the misery of that godforsaken country on the other side of the world.

Tired suddenly, of himself and the memories that threatened to swamp him, Lucas rolled his head around to relieve the stiffness in his neck and shoulders. Four months ago he'd turned thirty-six. He was disillusioned about many things, saddened by others, but, damn it all and despite everything, in charge of what his life had become. He was under no obligation to relive the mistakes of his youth, particularly not as they related to Emily. The days when they had been friends were long gone and there was no reason for their lives to interweave again now, no reason for the even tenor of his life to be disturbed—if, indeed, she was the one visiting Belvoir.

The thought brought him a measure of peace. Before turning from the window, he inhaled deeply one last time, filling his lungs with the scents of heliotrope and spring. But something else had crept in to spoil the purity of the night, something faintly acrid floating on the air and leaving it not quite as sweet as it had been moments before.

Suddenly alert, he snapped off the bedside lamp and leaned further out, eyes scanning, searching for he knew not what. Below, the river continued to flow softly. Above, the moon rode high above the trees that marked the boundary between Beatrice's property and the Lamartines'. God appeared to be in His heaven, and all right with the world, so who was Lucas Flynn to question otherwise?

He was about to turn away when a flicker of light through the trees, so brief he almost missed it, caught his eye, followed within seconds by a burst of orange.

Precious moments ticked by, moments of paralysed disbelief when he should have been responding to the emergency he wanted so badly to pretend wasn't taking place. And then he was sprinting for the door, calling out through the quiet house for Beatrice to wake up, to phone for help.

Ignoring Emily wasn't going to be quite as easy as he'd hoped. Because the Lamartine house was on fire.

CHAPTER TWO

EMILY surfaced from sleep slowly, reluctantly, the smell of the Alaska smoked cod Consuela had served for dinner connecting her vividly to the dream. Except that they'd had poached salmon for dinner and instead of fading, as dreams were supposed to, the odor winding in long, sinuous threads under her door was growing stronger, accompanied by a thin wail of distress from somewhere else in the house.

Suddenly wide awake, she bolted upright in the bed, her senses screaming a warning. Streaking across the room, she wrenched open the door, and found her worst fears confirmed by the blue haze of smoke rising in the stairwell.

"Grand-mère!" she cried, her voice echoing faintly, a whisper of dread. "Consuela!"

She raced into her grandmother's room. It was empty, the covers thrown back from the bed, and the sight terrified her. Belvoir was huge; it had eight bedrooms, all with connecting baths, and five reception rooms, in addition to the kitchen and breakfast room, then the entire third storey, which once had housed a fleet of servants but which Consuela now had to herself. Where did a person begin to search?

Was that her own pitiful little voice, whimpering with fear, that she could hear as she turned toward the upper floor? Was that really her, rooted to the spot and doing nothing to help Consuela as she tottered down the narrow upper stairs with her nightgown flapping around her feet and threatening to pitch her head-first onto the main landing?

"Dear Lord, she's done it again," Consuela said hoarsely, clutching her chest and fighting to draw breath.

It was enough to jolt Emily into full awareness. The crackle of flames had joined that poisonous column of smoke to underline the danger closing in on two infirm and helpless old women trapped in a house ablaze. If she was to get them and herself out safely, she had to take charge and fast. "My grandmother isn't in her room, Consuela. Do you know where she might—?"

Before she could complete the question, that wail of distress rose up from somewhere below on the main floor. Consuela heard it, too, and sighed with dull resignation. "*Madame* wanders..." she wheezed "...all over the place...when she can't sleep—"

"Never mind!" With uncivilized disregard for Consuela's age and lack of agility, Emily piloted her down the main staircase, driven by the knowledge that Monique was somewhere below, that she might be trapped by the flames or, worse yet, on fire herself. The possible outcome inherent in the situation didn't bear thinking about.

It was a nightmare journey. The smoke, thicker now, filled the stairwell, making their eyes smart, obscuring their vision, tormenting their lungs. Once, Consuela tripped on her long, flowing nightgown and almost tumbled both of them head over heels the rest of the way. But by some miracle she regained her balance and finally they rounded the last curve of the staircase. Emily knew because the arched entrance to the drawing room lay to the left, and the flames crawling up the draperies at the window within were turned to dazzling Catherine wheels of color by the smoke-induced tears stinging her eyes.

Directly ahead lay the front door and beyond it the sweet sanity of fresh air that her tortured lungs craved. "Almost there," she choked. "Just a couple more stairs, Consuela."

Blinded by smoke, she felt the newel post of the banister under her hand and knew she'd reached the bottom stair; knew that her next step would bring her to the solid floor of the entrance hall. She stretched out her foot, expecting to touch the smooth Italian marble tiles. And instead made contact with the crumpled heap that was her grandmother.

Did she open her mouth to scream? Was that what caused her lungs to rebel at the overload of smoke and leave her gagging as well as blinded? Was the noise that filled her ears the sound of her own panicked blood roaring through her veins—or the double front doors smashing open and urgent male voices shouting to each other?

It didn't matter. All that signified was the cool, firm grasp of another's hand, of the arm at her waist shepherding her out to where the blessedly pure night air waited to restore her breathing. Collapsing on the lawn, she watched through bleary, flooded eyes as the tall figure that had rescued her returned to Belvoir, and a moment later reappeared with her grandmother in his arms.

If she had thought that they might one day meet again, Emily had not expected that it would be like this, with them avoiding each other's eyes over Monique's prostrate figure. She had not thought she would owe him gratitude or thanks. Nor did he seem to expect it. Satisfied that her grandmother was breathing, Lucas Flynn turned back to help the other man, a stranger, who was bringing Consuela out through the door.

"Over here," he said, his voice full of quiet authority. "They're far enough away to be safe here for now." His gaze came to rest on Emily and just briefly, in the midst of the panic and fear, a spark of awareness more dangerous than the fire within the house flared between them. And then it was gone, doused by the blank indifference in his blue eyes. "Is there anyone else inside?" he asked.

She shook her head and held a hand to her painful throat. "No."

"No pets or anything?"

How could she have forgotten her grandmother's beloved, bad-tempered Robespierre? "There's the cat—"

"He goes hunting," Consuela wheezed, "every night. There is no one left inside."

The other man, the stranger, spoke kindly. "Where's your garden hose? The blaze seems confined to one room so perhaps I can put it out or at least contain it."

"Don't try going in there again," Lucas said shortly. "Acting the hero isn't going to help if you end up another casualty. That's the last thing we need."

"I'll break the window and work from the outside." The stranger's manner was quietly confident, the hand he rested on Emily's shoulder sympathetic. "We can't stand by watching family treasures go up in smoke without doing something about it, now can we?"

"Suit yourself," Lucas muttered, squatting beside Monique and checking her pulse.

After a moment, he sat back on his heels and blew out a breath. Without thinking, Emily reached out and touched his arm. If she'd grasped a live wire, the jolt could not have shocked her more. Snatching back her hand, she said, "How is she?"

"Better than either of you, it seems," he replied, jerking a nod at Consuela who lay like a sack of flour, panting audibly.

His impersonal tone and the way he refused to look at her left Emily feeling like an interloper. Annoyed, she said as sharply as her beleaguered lungs would allow, "How can that be? She was passed out on the floor."

"Exactly," he replied loftily, as if only a complete fool would fail to figure it out for herself, "and smoke rises. She's suffered almost no harmful inhalation."

Monique chose that moment to assert herself. "I did not pass out," she announced in distinct tones that left

no one in any doubt about her umbrage at being treated
as if she weren't quite all there. "I slipped and fell."

"Did you?" he said impassively. "And how are you
feeling now?"

"Like hell, Lucas Flynn, and if you were any sort of
doctor you'd know that without having to ask."

Unperturbed, he began to examine her, probing gently
along her neck and down her arms. "Want to tell me
how you came to fall?"

"I was trying to alert my household to the fact that
my home was on fire."

"How do you think it started?"

"I have no idea," she returned frostily.

"It was the same as before," Consuela said.
"*Madame —*"

"Be quiet!" Monique snapped. "How could you
possibly know anything when you were upstairs snoring
so loudly that I couldn't sleep?"

Just then Beatrice Flynn, Lucas's grandmother, came
traipsing through the trees, clad in a brocade dressing
gown and with her hair hanging down her back in a long
gray braid. "Praise the Lord Lucas got you out alive!"
she cried, the beam of the flashlight she carried swinging
in a wide arc over them where they huddled on the lawn.
"You could all have fried in your beds!"

"You must be terribly disappointed," Monique retorted with a malevolent glare.

"That's a wicked thing to say, Monique Lamartine.
I wouldn't wish anyone dead, not even you."

Perhaps it was as well that the sound of sirens split
the night just then, signaling the arrival of emergency
vehicles and thus preventing another round in the years-
old feud between the two dowagers.

"Three casualties, none too serious," Lucas informed
the ambulance attendants, while the fire marshall or-
ganized his crew. "This one had a stroke recently, the

other two suffered some smoke inhalation. A night in the hospital won't hurt any of them."

"I do not require hospitalization," Monique declared, struggling to sit up, "but by all means take Consuela. She's wheezing like a locomotive."

"This hasn't been easy on you either, Mrs. Lamartine," he said as the paramedics loaded Consuela onto a stretcher. "You need rest and a thorough check-up, too."

"You're supposed to be a doctor and you've just given me a check-up. How many more do I need?"

"You'll be better cared for in a properly equipped medical center."

"No," she said, waving aside his concern. "This is my home and here I intend to remain."

"That's impossible, as I'm sure you know," Lucas replied, with thinly veiled impatience. "If you refuse to follow my advice then you'll have to find some other place to stay because there's no way you'll be allowed back into your house tonight, nor, I suspect, for some time to come."

"You're quite right," Emily said. "Grand-mère, we'll phone for a taxi and take a room at the hotel, then in the morning I'll contact the family and make temporary arrangements for you to stay with—"

"You will do no such thing, Emily Jane! Furthermore, if you attempt to use this unfortunate incident to convince me that my children are correct in thinking I'm unable to care for myself without their help, then not only are you a dreadful disappointment to me, are you also no longer welcome in my home."

"Well, she's welcome in mine," Beatrice put in. "And so, come to that, are you, Monique Lamartine, though why I should put myself out for you I don't know. It's a miserable old woman you've become, and I pray I don't turn out the same when I'm your age."

"You're already my age and then some!"

Beatrice did an about-turn and prepared to march back the way she'd come. "I'll not waste breath arguing with you. If my house isn't good enough, you can sleep under the stars for all I care. Emily Jane, if you decide to take me up on my offer, you know where I live."

She was almost at the boundary of the two properties when Monique called out grudgingly, "I never said your house wasn't good enough, you silly woman."

Beatrice spun around in her tracks. "Are you saying you'd like me to prepare a room for you, then?" she inquired, exacting a full measure of revenge in the way she pointedly waited for a reply.

Emily could have sworn she saw her grandmother swallow the huge chunk of pride threatening to choke her before she managed, "Under these very unusual circumstances, I find that an acceptable alternative, yes."

"In that case," Beatrice said, "I'll ask you, Lucas, to fetch the car round so that poor, feeble Mrs. Lamartine doesn't have to trek through the woods at such an ungodly hour and her in nothing but a soot-stained nightie."

Even outdoors, with people and space between them, Emily felt his presence too acutely. The idea of finding herself confined with him in the close quarters of a car, even for the short time it would take him to drive them next door, filled her with dismay.

Apparently, Lucas felt likewise. "Of course," he said, politely enough, his eyes resting on Emily, but then his gaze flicked away from her as if she were nothing but the unpleasant figment of someone else's imagination.

Beatrice assigned her to the second guest suite, a big square room with a sitting alcove at one end and an en suite bathroom at the other. She had laid out a long cotton gown which, while it was certainly several sizes too large, was infinitely preferable to Emily's own grass-stained, smoke-drenched nightshirt. That and the deep tub lured her to delay the pleasure of crawling between the sweet-smelling sheets until she'd shampooed her hair and soaped her skin clean of the fire's residue.

She had just emerged from the bathroom with her hair turbaned in a towel when a tap came at the bedroom door. "Emily Jane, darling, are you in bed yet?" Beatrice called softly.

"Not quite," Emily said. "Come in, Mrs. Flynn."

"I'll not disturb you," Beatrice said, popping her head around the door. "I just want to make sure you have everything you need. Also, I've made cocoa, and if you're ready for it I'll bring it up to you."

"You'll do no such thing," Emily said, walking over to the door and opening it wider. "It might be over ten years since I was last here, but I haven't forgotten where the kitchen is and you've been disturbed enough for one night. Go to bed, please, or before you know it it'll be time to get up again."

"Well, I will, then, if it's all the same to you." Beatrice took Emily's hands affectionately. "It's a lovely woman you've grown into, Emily Jane, and I've missed you. Don't let another ten years go by before you come to stay again."

Was it being assailed by yet another shock, the after-effects of smoke or plain and simple fatigue that had Emily's eyes threatening to fill with tears? "You were always so kind to us, Mrs. Flynn, despite..."

Beatrice knew what she meant. The ill-will between the grandmothers had been as much a part of everyday life as the river flowing past the bottom of their gardens. "And why would I not be? Two silly old women feuding over the Lord knows what have no business putting innocent children in the way of their bickering."

Emily experienced a flash of guilt at that. How innocent had she been the night she'd tried to bring her romantic dreams to fruition? But if her grandmother held

Lucas responsible for the outcome it was obvious from
Beatrice's attitude that she either remained ignorant of
the true order of events or else chose not to assign blame.

"Make yourself at home and sleep as long as you like
in the morning, darling," she said, planting a kiss on
Emily's cheek. "There's no rush to be up and about.
We'll look after your grandma for you; never doubt
that."

When Emily stole downstairs fifteen minutes later, the
air was filled with the hush of a house at rest and nothing
but the quiet tick of clocks to mark the passing hours.
Except for a ray of light spilling out of the kitchen into
the downstairs hall, the rooms lay in darkness.

Despite the addition of two built-in convection wall
ovens and a dishwasher, the kitchen hadn't changed
much over the years. The same scrubbed pine table still
occupied the middle of the red tiled floor, the copper
pots still hung from a circular rack above it, and if the
geraniums flowering on the windowsill above the sink
weren't the ones that had flourished in her childhood
Emily couldn't have told the difference.

She ought to have considered that he might also be in
the room. Even if the theory of feminine intuition was
based on nothing but a lot of wishful thinking, sheer
common sense should have warned her, when she saw
the tray containing a Thermos and two saucers but only
one cup, that she was not alone.

But it was the shiny chrome surface of the Thermos
that alerted her to his presence, mirroring his reflection
as he stirred from his spot by the big, old-fashioned fireplace. And by then it was too late to pretend she hadn't
seen him, too late to worry that she looked ridiculous
in the voluminous nightgown that had been in fashion
at least fifty years before and whose hem she held hiked
up around her knees, and much too late to rehearse this
first private meeting with him since the night she'd

slithered, uninvited, between the sheets of his bed and seduced him.

For a while it appeared that neither of them was willing to break the silence unspooling between them. Instead, they simply stared at each other, he remotely, like the stranger he undoubtedly wished he were, and she—ye gods, her gaze clung to him shamelessly, devouring his every feature with the rapacity of a woman on the brink of starvation.

In the more revealing light of the kitchen, she could see what had not been so apparent in the gloom of Belvoir's garden. He had aged, but so graciously that he was even more beautiful than he'd been at twenty-five. His hair lay as thick and unruly as ever, the only difference being that now it was lightly shot with silver.

As for his mouth...! Oh, despite the hardships he might have known, his mouth was as she'd always remembered it, so blatantly sexy that her lips parted in mute supplication to know its touch again.

Just once more, her wayward heart cried. Just once and it'll be enough. I'll never ask again.

Appalled, she said primly, "If I'd realized you were down here—"

"You'd have remained upstairs." He offered the merest suggestion of a shrug. "I could say the same thing but it would be pointless, wouldn't it? You're here, I'm here, and it seems that whether we like it or not we're destined to acknowledge each other."

She wished he hadn't moved his shoulders in that sinuous way that drew attention less to their width, which had always been impressive, than to the fact that his shirt was unbuttoned and hanging loose at the waist of his blue jeans. Her gaze dropped from his mouth to the expanse of flesh that his gesture had uncovered.

The musculature of his chest was more defined than when she'd run her hands over its planes that other summer, the skin even more deeply tanned. His stomach, though, was the same: flat and hard, just as it had been then. Except for his mouth and his hands, he had been hard all over that night...

"I was going to say I wouldn't have disturbed you," she said, corralling her thoughts before they got her into more trouble than she could possibly cope with. "We've put you to enough trouble already, getting you out of bed to rush to our rescue."

"I'm a night owl. I'm seldom asleep before one or two in the morning."

You were the night I came sneaking in, she thought. You were out cold, lying with nothing but a sheet covering you, and it took me no time at all to whisk it aside and confirm every last delicious fantasy I'd ever harbored about you.

Her sharply drawn breath escaped before she could suppress it. Face flaming, she swung back to the Thermos of cocoa and hoped her hands wouldn't betray her by shaking too visibly as she filled the lone cup.

The worst was over, surely? They'd come face to face, exchanged the barest civilities and both survived the ordeal. Now all she had to do was beat a not too obvious retreat before her unruly memory betrayed her more than it already had.

"How have you been, Emily?"

Instead of being fielded from across the kitchen, his question flowed over her shoulder, and she realized that he'd moved to stand close behind her. Much too close. Agitated, she sought refuge around the other side of the table. "Very well, thank you."

"And your husband?"

"Husband?"

A smile settled fleetingly on his mouth, a glimmer of cool white amusement against the bronze of his skin. "The man you married."

"I—he's well, too." Even had this been the time and place to divulge that her marriage was a thing of the past, Lucas Flynn was not the one to burden with the disclosure. It wasn't as if he gave a damn; he was merely going through the socially correct motions, as was she when she said, "I was sorry to hear about your wife."

He lifted his shoulders in another dismissive shrug. "These things happen," he said, so dispassionately that Emily couldn't help but wonder if he'd ousted Sydney from his life as easily as he'd evicted her.

"You make it sound as if her death was more inconvenient than tragic," she heard herself remark acidly.

Annoyance thinned his lips, his amusement dispelled so thoroughly that, if memory hadn't served her better, she'd have thought him incapable of smiling. "I hardly feel I have to justify to you how I choose to deal with personal tragedy, Emily Jane."

"You never felt you had to justify anything to me!" The last thing she'd wanted was to be the one to resurrect the past. Even less did she want to come across as the woman wronged, particularly since she'd been the aggressor in their encounter, but the words were out before she could stop them, full of accusation and reproach.

He expelled a brief sigh. "I had hoped you'd forgotten," he said. "I can't imagine why you'd want to hang onto the memory."

Of course he couldn't, because he hadn't been the one to offer his heart and have it tossed back without a word of appreciation or thanks. He'd walked away untouched, whereas she'd been permanently scarred by her botched attempt to make him love her as she'd loved him.

He had no idea, no idea at all, of the ultimate cost to her of the night she'd seduced him. Blissfully ignorant, he'd gone forward, married the woman of his choice, and left Emily to carry the burden of her guilt and sorrow alone. Knowing he hadn't been to blame for that didn't prevent her from resenting him for it.

"I don't," she replied stonily. "As a matter of fact, I haven't thought about you in years until today."

"Then you've been happy?"

"What do you care?" Oh, Emily, shut up! she told herself angrily.

His sigh this time was fraught with exasperation, as if he found having to explain such obvious and simple facts exceedingly tedious. "We were friends for a long time, Emily. Closer than friends, even. More like brother and sister. One night of...indiscretion doesn't negate all the good times. Of course I care."

About as much as he cared about the weather! But he wasn't her brother, she didn't want his diluted affection, and she couldn't bear his bold references to a time she'd truly tried to bury in the past where it belonged. She wanted to escape and shut herself in her room, to be alone before she faced the fact that he still had the power to affect her more deeply than any other man she'd ever met.

"Then, to answer your question, I am very happy, very successful, and very tired," she said, stepping around him and heading for the door. "Thank you again for coming to our rescue tonight. Under the circumstances, it was very decent of you."

"Decent?" Although she couldn't see it this time, she heard the amusement in his voice. "What else could I have done? Left you to burn?"

"You might have, if you'd known I was visiting my grandmother."

"Hardly," he scoffed. "I took a professional oath a long time ago to preserve and honor human life."

It was on the tip of her tongue to ask, Even mine? but she bit back the words and said instead, "Of course. Well, don't worry that we'll make a habit of calling on you to bail us out of trouble. We pride ourselves on being very self-sufficient."

* * *

Like every other assertion she'd made in the last little
while, however, that last one of Emily's turned out to
be erroneous. By the following morning, Monique's left
knee was badly swollen. "I remember twisting it when
I slipped," she admitted to Lucas when, at Beatrice's
insistence, he came to take a look.

"If you had gone to the hospital to be checked over
as I suggested, this could have been taken care of last
night," he pointed out.

"With everything else that was happening at the time,
it didn't seem worth mentioning. In any case, you're
supposed to be a doctor so you can take care of it now."

"I'm not leaving myself open to your suing me for
negligence, Mrs. Lamartine," he informed her. "For a
start, I have no malpractice insurance, and second, I
don't need the aggravation. Whether you like it or not,
you're going into town for X-rays. And consider yourself
lucky you didn't break a hip."

"If this is an example of your bedside manner, it's no
wonder you had to give up practicing medicine,"
Monique retorted.

Earlier, Emily had gone over to Belvoir to meet the
fire marshall and hear his report on last night's disaster.
Although he'd allowed her to collect a few clothes and
other basic necessities, he'd been adamant that the house
was not safe in its present condition.

The drawing room, sadly, was destroyed, its furnishings blackened and soaked in water, and there had
been structural damage to a supporting wall. Not surprisingly, the whole house also reeked of smoke. It would
be weeks before they could go home again—news which
Emily knew would not be well received.

In her view, all this was trouble enough for one day.
She certainly didn't need to run interference when
Monique decided to bait Lucas—which was every chance
she got. She had enough to do holding her own emotions in check where he was concerned.

"I'll get you to the hospital," she offered, hoping to distract her grandmother. "They phoned this morning to let us know that Consuela is ready to come home, so I have to drop by anyway, with a change of clothes for her and to collect her. Then, once you're taken care of, we'll go over to the hotel and take a suite there until we decide what to do next."

"Whatever for?" Beatrice exclaimed, coming into the room just in time to hear the tail end of the conversation. "There's plenty of room here for all of you without us falling over one another."

"You're very kind," Monique said grandly, "but it would be an imposition and so quite out of the question."

"Don't be so quick to turn me down," Beatrice said. "We're heading into summer and the tourists are pouring into the area already. Suppose they can't take you at the hotel? Where'll you go then, Monique Lamartine, since you're so dead set against burdening your family with your ill-tempered presence? Somehow, I don't see you camping in a tent until your poor house is fit to live in again."

"Phone for a taxi, Emily Jane," Monique said, with lofty disdain for such pitiful reasoning. "We have business to which we must attend and I would like it concluded as speedily as possible."

Beatrice opened her mouth to object to that idea too, but Lucas forestalled her with weary resignation. "I'll drive you into town."

"Thank you, but no," Emily said. "That really is asking too much."

"Not at all. I've got a number of errands to attend to." He finished the last of his coffee and checked his watch. "If you could be ready to leave in half an hour?"

For all that he phrased them so politely, the words were a command, not a request, and underlined what he'd made patently clear the night before: their presence, particularly Emily's, was an imposition of the highest order.

When they arrived at the hospital just after eleven, the first person they spoke to was Monique's doctor, whose opinion, when he heard about the previous night's events, coincided entirely with Lucas's. Rapping out orders, he whisked his patient into a wheelchair and off for a complete physical, including an X-ray of her knee.

"Barring any unusual findings, you should be able to pick her up in about three hours," he told Emily over his shoulder as he pushed aside the swinging doors through which her grandmother had already disappeared.

Lucas, who'd accompanied them inside the building, spoke for the first time. "That'll give me plenty of time to take care of my business, so unless there's something else I can do for you I'll take off now and meet you back here around two."

Without waiting for a reply, he did precisely that, disappearing with what Emily perceived to be enormous relief at being rid of them. She, however, was alarmed at the length of time her grandmother was to be detained.

"Does it normally take three hours to run a few tests?" she asked the nurse who'd assisted with Monique's preliminary examination. "Or is the doctor concerned that my grandmother might have had another stroke, do you think?"

"Well, he'll want to make sure that hasn't happened, of course, but it's more a precautionary measure. Also, things slow down a bit over the lunch hour so we don't always get test results back as quickly as we'd like." The nurse smiled reassuringly. "Hanging around the emergency unit's enough to give anyone the willies and the food in the cafeteria is lousy. Why don't you treat yourself to lunch in town? It's a much pleasanter way to pass the time."

But not the most efficient, Emily decided, particularly with the question of where they were all going to live for the next little while still unresolved.

It turned out not to be a problem for Consuela. "No hotel for me, Miss Emily," she declared, accepting the clothes Emily had brought for her to wear. "My sister-in-law's been asking me to pay a visit for months, so now I will. When *madame's* ready for me to come back to work, she can phone. I'm just across town and can be out to Belvoir in no time at all."

"Well, at least let me see you off in a taxi," Emily said.

"It was the cigarettes, you know," Consuela confided some twenty minutes later, while they waited for the elevator. "*Madame* won't admit it but it's a miracle she hasn't brought the house down about our ears before last night. She falls asleep while she's smoking, you see."

Her account confirmed what the fire marshall had stated in his report. "I'm sorry you've had to deal with the worry of it all by yourself, Consuela," Emily said. "What you're telling me now merely reinforces what I've already decided. We're going to have to look at a better arrangement once Belvoir is fit to live in again. Meantime, we'll be at the hotel if you need us for anything."

But Beatrice appeared to have been blessed with divine foresight, because the April Water Hotel—the only hotel in town—could give them a room for two nights only. After that, the place was pretty well booked for the remainder of the season. Any hope of securing long-term residence was out of the question. Nor were any of the quaint bed-and-breakfast houses able to help. They didn't cater for full-time guests.

It seemed that avoiding Lucas wasn't going to pan out quite as neatly or quickly as Emily had hoped. Unless a miracle occurred within the next hour or two, she and

Monique might have no choice but to accept Beatrice's hospitality until Belvoir was habitable again.

The thought of having to face Lucas across the dining-room table three times a day, not to mention running into him at other times in between, and of sleeping down the hall from him, left her dizzy with dismay.

CHAPTER THREE

IT SEEMED prophetic that the first person Emily ran into on the street after she'd seen Consuela off was Lucas. He'd just crossed the road from the post office, which was situated opposite the entrance to the hospital, and was so busy thumbing through the mail he'd picked up that he quite literally cannoned into her. "Sorry," he muttered absently, reaching out a hand to steady her, then did a double-take when he realized who it was he'd almost knocked down.

For just a second, she was reminded of the day she'd fallen in love with him. He'd almost stumbled over her then, too, and a whole sequence of events had been set in motion. One kiss had led to another and she'd read "for ever" in them. Sadly, she'd been the only one to do so. She'd also been pathologically naive in those days.

"Good thing it wasn't your grandmother," he said now, the ghost of his old self emerging briefly. "She'd be threatening lawsuits for sure. So, did you get fixed up at the hotel?"

"No," Emily said, dry-mouthed all over again at the sheer male magnificence of him.

He had no right to be so beautiful. He was too muscular in the chest and shoulders for a doctor, as if he'd spent the last eleven years in some work more physically strenuous than she could envision medicine being. He should have been stooped and the African sun should have left his skin all wizened. His eyes should have faded, been half-buried in wrinkles from squinting in the bright, tropical light; they should have peered out myopically through thick lenses. Instead, he was spellbinding, his

40

lean-hipped, rangy grace lending elegance even to the blue jeans that seemed to be his preferred mode of dress these days.

"No?" He *did* have squint lines around his eyes when he glanced at her quizzically like that, but they were an asset, enhancing his good looks rather than detracting from them.

She shook her head. "Your grandmother was right. Except for a couple of days here and there, the hotel's booked up right through September."

If he was dismayed to hear that, he hid it well. "From Monique's standpoint that might not be such a bad thing, you know. It's my guess she's damaged the ligaments in her knee and that she'll be off her feet for the next week or so. Being confined to a hotel room would be no picnic for anyone, especially not someone of her...ah... temperament."

"I'm afraid," Emily said, wondering how many times she was going to have to apologize to him for one thing or another, "that she's behaving very ungraciously toward you and your grandmother, and I'm sorry. I think it's just that she's afraid of change, of not being in control of the events shaping her life. What with her failing health and now this latest problem, she sees her independence seeping away, and it terrifies her, but she's too proud to admit it."

He rubbed his chin thoughtfully. "Growing old can be hell, Emily, and some people react just as your grandmother does, fighting it every step of the way."

"Still, that's no reason for you to have to put up with her ill humor."

When he laughed, the years melted away from his face, leaving only the threads of silver in his hair to betray his true age. "I might as well get used to it. It looks as if we're all stuck with each other—at least for the next little while."

"Stuck with each other? Oh, I don't think so!"

"You have some other solution up your sleeve?"

"Well, I...no, not exactly—not yet. How could I, when I only just found out the hotel can't take us? But I'll come up with something."

"I can't imagine what. Your grandmother made it plain enough last night that she's not budging far from home. And quite frankly, even if the idea of moving in with relatives did sit well with her, I doubt her doctor wants to see her traveling any great distance right now. She's a lot frailer than she might seem, you know."

"So what are you saying? That the only other choice is...?" She lapsed into silence, still unwilling to accept the solution staring her in the face.

Entertaining no such uncertainty, Lucas finished the question for her. "Roscommon? Afraid so." Another of those brief smiles illuminated his face. "Don't look so horrified, Emily. We don't have rats in the pantry or bugs in the beds, and, although it might not be her home, realistically it's probably the best place for Monique to be right now. She'll be on relatively familiar territory, able to keep an eye on repairs to Belvoir, voice her disapproval of everything the workmen do—which will keep her happy even if it does run them ragged!—and at the same time give my grandmother someone else to bully besides me."

His summation was right on target: sensible, practical, convenient. But Emily was too dismayed to acknowledge any of those supremely sane responses—so dismayed, in fact, that she blurted out her true thoughts without taking time to edit them first or consider how they might be interpreted. "Lucas, I couldn't possibly stay another night under the same roof as you!"

She hadn't meant to sound so insulting but he allowed her no time to rephrase her objection. His eyes narrowed, their brilliant blue stripped of any amusement. "Why not?" he drawled. "Forewarned is forearmed. I have a lock on my bedroom door and I'll make a point of using it.''

She had thought he could never hurt her again, that nothing could come close to the pure agony of having him reject her and turn to another woman for all those things *she* had been willing to give him. But his softly uttered contempt seared her more thoroughly than anything he'd flung at her the night she'd conceived his child. Devastated, she spun away from him, stepping blindly off the edge of the sidewalk and out into the road.

A horn blared, brakes shrieked. The bright red fender of a car reared up and seemed to hover perilously close as she stumbled to regain her balance.

I'm going to be killed, she thought in mild surprise, and wondered who'd come in her place to take care of Monique.

And then Lucas's hand shot out, grabbing her urgently by the scruff of the neck and yanking her back to safety. Or increased danger, depending on one's perspective. Because finding herself pressed up against him, pressed so close that they were imprinted on each other from knee to breast, was just as life-threatening in a different kind of way.

For the first time since they'd met again, his eyes neither avoided hers nor skittered past her as if the sight of her was too repugnant to be endured. Instead, his gaze burned into her, ablaze with impassioned horror. To the people passing by, they might have appeared to be lovers locked in wordless conflict, so furiously did he clutch her to him.

But they weren't lovers. And the fact that, even knowing that, she still wanted to lean into him, to bury her face in his neck and inhale the warm, well-remembered scent of him, enraged her.

So she shrugged him off and flicked at her hair to restore it to some sort of order. "Do you *mind?*" she said, too discombobulated to care that, considering he'd just spared her serious injury and possibly even saved her life, the question was downright ridiculous.

Lucas passed a trembling hand over his face. "Damned right," he said hoarsely. "Jeez, Emily, if you want to teach me to think before I speak in future, a smack in the mouth will suffice, OK? You don't have to lay your life on the line to make your point."

She allowed him a small smile, then looked away. Just as well. It would never have done for her to see how shaken up he was, how close to losing it, and all because of her. How could he have explained such a reaction when he didn't understand it himself?

It wasn't as if the car had actually touched her. In fact, it had squealed to a halt a good six feet away. It was those seconds in between that had left him such a mess. One minute she'd been standing there, perfect in pale green linen and straw accessories, clearly repelled by the thought of living in the same house with him, breathing the same air, and the next he'd retaliated with a blow so low it was unforgivable, and the damage was done.

She'd blanched with shock. Her eyes had seemed to fill her face, huge brown wells of pain, and her mouth had opened in a perfect, soundless pink O, leaving him feeling as if he'd just kicked a puppy in the teeth. Then, before he could begin to form an apology, she'd swung around in a graceful arc and floated out of his reach and practically under the wheels of the passing car.

"Lucas?" She was looking at him again and rubbing absently at the back of her neck where he'd grabbed hold of her.

"What? Did I hurt you?"

She lifted one elegant shoulder in a ghost of a shrug. "Not really. But this other business—about us living at Roscommon until Belvoir's been repaired—how can it possibly work, Lucas, with things the way they are between us?"

"What say I buy you lunch and we'll talk about it? We've still got a couple of hours to kill before we collect Grandma."

"I'm not very hungry."

She looked a bit pale and more than a little apprehensive, as though the potential pitfalls of such a living arrangement were more than she could face. "Then you can watch me eat while we deal with all the history between us," he said, "because the way things are shaping up we aren't going to be able to avoid each other for the next little while. And although I can't speak for you, Emily Jane, I don't mind admitting that it's going to be rough going for me unless we clear the air a bit."

"All right, whatever you say," she muttered.

He took her to a restaurant overlooking the April river. From the front it was nothing but a narrow, brick-faced building with a canopied entrance and a wrought iron railing, but inside it opened onto a long courtyard with a fountain in the middle and a profusion of flowering plants spilling down the walls and over the edges of ceramic containers.

They were shown to a table on the south side, shaded by a tilted sun umbrella. Disregarding what she'd said about not being hungry, Lucas ordered for both of them—fish chowder with sourdough bread, and iced tea. "So," he began, immediately the waiter left, "do you want to start the ball rolling, or shall I?"

"You," she said unhesitatingly.

"OK." He took a swig of iced tea. "The way I see it, you and I got off track the last summer we spent here."

"No." She shook her head. "It happened long before that, Lucas. It all began the summer I turned fifteen and you kissed me for the first time. Or are you going to pretend you've forgotten about that?"

He stirred the lemon wedge around in his glass and wished he could look her in the eye and lie. It had been such a brief incident, after all, hardly one to hang onto through the years. But, "No," he admitted, expelling a long breath. "I remember only too well."

"Why did you do it, Lucas? Kiss me, I mean?"

"Why?" He lifted his shoulders, feigning bafflement. "Don't ask me. It wasn't something I planned. Hell, you'd always been just another of the cousins from next door, all pigtails and big brown eyes. The kid I'd taught to swim when she was about five. Then you...changed."

"Are you saying it was my fault that time, too?"

In a way, yes, he thought, but he could hardly come out and tell her that, over the preceding winter, she'd grown into a leggy adolescent with breasts. Or that they had been the first thing he'd noticed when she'd come to Belvoir that particular summer.

A couple of his brothers had noticed, too. "Emily Jane's grown hooters," fifteen-year old Sean had whispered, bug-eyed with awe. "Man, hand me my catcher's mitt!"

Ted, who at seventeen had thought himself vastly more experienced in such matters, had scoffed, "They're not big enough to fill a bra let alone a baseball glove. Save your energy, kid!"

But Lucas, who'd turned twenty the previous November and had, at their age, been prone to much the same kind of irreverence, had known an inexplicable urge to flatten both brothers. Feigning lofty indifference, he'd stalked inside to catch up on the reading requirements for his second year of university, due to start that September.

"It wasn't your fault," he said now.

"Well, thank you for that much," she said. "Particularly since I remember that summer as being one of the happiest I spent at Belvoir."

"For me too," he admitted. And it was true, up to a point. As the days had gone by, the phenomenon of Emily's breasts had gradually ceased to elicit wonder among the brothers at Roscommon House and by the middle of August the old, easy camaraderie between the younger members of the two families had re-established itself.

"It marked the end of an era," he went on. "We were never that carefree again."

"No." Her voice was soft, her brown eyes hazy, as though pictures from that summer were unrolling in her mind. "We clowned around every day, shoving each other off the end of the diving pier or cannonballing into the river, and sat around a bonfire nearly every night. One big, happy family, with no hidden agendas or undercurrents to spoil things."

"Until the night I kissed you," Lucas said. "Nothing was ever the same after that. It was the last day of the summer vacation, as I recall, and the last year that we were all together like that. We'd gone swimming after dark, my brothers and I, and you and all your cousins from Belvoir, and we were making one hell of a noise."

"And your grandmother came out and hammered on the old ship's bell hanging from the back porch of Roscommon, and told us to get inside before we were all arrested for disturbing the peace!"

"She bribed us with gingerbread and fruit punch," he said.

"Right. And in the rush to get up to the house I slipped and fell among the reeds lining the river bank."

And he'd been right behind her and had leaned down and yanked her to her feet more roughly than he'd meant to, and somehow she had crashed into him, and he'd had his arms around her to steady her, and she'd looked up at him with her big brown eyes and her lips had been parted and shining with water....

"And that's when you kissed me."

"Yes," he said, memory rushing back.

He'd kissed other girls before. Older, more experienced girls. Done a bit more than kiss them, if truth be known. But none had tasted like her, as cool and fresh as dew, and none had responded with such artless sensuality. Before he'd had time to consider the wisdom of it—

"And then you kissed me again."

He hadn't been able to help himself. She'd swayed toward him, pressing her sweet little breasts against his chest, and he'd found himself suddenly and furiously aroused. Horrified—because this was Emily Jane, after all, the kid who was like a sister—he'd shoved her away. "Here," he'd said gruffly, flinging a towel at her and camouflaging himself with another at the same time. "And watch where you're stepping in future."

Ice cubes clinked musically, and he looked up to find Emily watching him over the rim of her glass. "You left Roscommon the next day without saying goodbye," she said.

He scowled. "Pity I didn't leave a day earlier."

"I take that to mean you didn't find kissing me a particularly pleasant experience."

"I was out of line, crass—immoral, even, taking advantage of a kid your age and losing my self-respect in the process. I had no business laying a hand on you."

"Don't beat yourself up over it, Lucas. It *was* only a kiss—or two, to be exact. It wasn't your fault they meant the whole world to me at the time. I was just a moon-struck adolescent who'd never been kissed like that before."

"But if I'd shown more restraint then, you might not have thought...we might not have—" Exasperated, he shoved his bowl of chowder aside and leaned back in his chair. "For crying out loud, wouldn't you think a medical doctor would be able to spit out the words without stammering and floundering like a kid caught looking at dirty pictures?"

He took a deep breath and started over again. "If I'd had the good sense to maintain the status quo in our relationship when you were fifteen, we might never have made the mistake of becoming intimate when you were nineteen. If I didn't say so at the time, I want you to know now that I deeply regret the way things...turned out, and hold myself entirely responsible.''

When she didn't answer, he leaned forward again and reached for her hands. ''You do know that, don't you, Emily Jane?''

She couldn't bear any of it, not the intensity of his gaze as he squinted at her through the thick black lashes framing his beautiful eyes, not his fingers curling warmly around hers, not the pretty, intimate restaurant, not his knee almost brushing hers under the table. They were all things that could have spelled romance and happy ever after, except those two items were not on the menu today.

''I wish you wouldn't keep tacking the Jane on my name,'' she snapped. ''I outgrew it a long time ago, even if I can't convince my grandmother that's so. But coming from you—'' She drew an irate breath. ''Well, it merely underlines the fact that you still think of me as that same silly girl who...who behaved so foolishly.''

''I never thought of you as silly, and as for still seeing you as a girl...'' His gaze swept over her again, more thoroughly. ''You're hardly that, Emily,'' he sighed, ''and that's half the problem.''

She could no more quell the surge of hope that his admission evoked than she could have stopped the sun from rising. ''Are you saying things would be different now if we were to—?''

He reared back in his seat as if he'd discovered a rattlesnake in his soup. ''Hell, no!''

She was such a fool! Such a beggar for punishment! ''In that case,'' she said snippily, ''I'd appreciate your finding some other way of clearing the air because trying to flatter me into falling in with whatever you've got planned isn't going to work.''

"I'm not trying to flatter you. I'm merely stating the obvious. You're too sophisticated not to know that you're a beautiful woman, that you turn heads when you walk down the street—stop traffic, even!"

He grinned briefly, disarmingly, then sobered quickly as he got to what he really wanted to say. "But none of that has anything to do with the fact that there's this big, ugly secret between us and I think we have to agree to lay it to rest, once and for all—agree that it was regrettable but that it *is* over and best forgotten. We were never lovers, never romantically involved, and we never will be. We're simply two people who knew each other a long time ago."

Was it the combination of too many shocks following too close one after the other that made her want to moan with pain and outrage at his callous dismissal of the most glorious and, ultimately, most devastating night of her life?

I gave you my virginity and my innocence, she wanted to howl. Wasn't it enough that you threw them back at me, that I dealt with the loss of our child and never asked anything of you? Do you have to rub salt in the wounds by making it plain you've never harbored a moment's desire for me?

"Emily?" His voice murmured across the table, full of concern. "Did you hear me?"

She tried to blink into focus the wavering shape of the glass in front of her. "Oh, yes," she said bitterly. "You have a real talent for destroying a person's illusions with your choice of words. You might remember that night as nothing but one 'big, ugly secret' but I have quite a different perception."

He leaned toward her. "You had a crush on me and got carried away by it. I blame myself for not seeing that things were headed toward disaster and steering you clear of it. My only excuse is that I really thought, with all the talk about Sydney coming to Roscommon to meet

Beatrice, that you understood how things stood between me and her.''

"All I knew about you and Sydney was that you were both medical students. I thought he was a man," Emily said, long past the point of caring that her voice and demeanor betrayed the anguish consuming her. "It never occurred to me that you'd make love to me one night and then introduce some other woman as your fiancée two days later."

"I didn't 'make love' to you!" Lucas whispered, suddenly furious enough to have no trouble at all speaking plainly. "We rolled around between the sheets and ended up having sex. There was no love involved, not on your part, not on mine, and if you remember it any differently you're lying to yourself."

"Am I really!" she spat back, lashing out at him now for the pain she'd suffered then. "Well, tell me this, Dr. High-And-Mighty-Know-It-All: was the rabbit also lying when it died?"

CHAPTER FOUR

For a stunned moment, neither of them moved or spoke. Lucas seemed paralyzed, and as for Emily—she had done the unforgivable. She had taken the one secret she'd sworn to protect and cherish at any price, and flung it into the arena just to punish him. She'd left behind her pride and self-respect that awful night, and now she'd tossed aside the only thing of worth she'd brought away with her: the unborn child who had been hers to know and love for such a short while.

And the disgraceful part of it was, she couldn't be sorry. Instead she dissolved into giggles. She couldn't help herself because, as the import of her words finally sank home, Lucas's reaction was just too priceless.

At first, he simply stared at her, as if she'd grown three heads, then, "You were *pregnant*?" he said, his tone all hushed, the way people's were at funerals.

"What did you think I meant?" she taunted him between snickers. "That I'd gone into the fur coat business?"

At that, he dropped his fork, he dropped his jaw, and he dropped his "I'm in charge and this is the way things are going to be done around here" act. Dropped all three so damned fast that she split her sides laughing.

So did everyone else in the restaurant. Through the tears gushing from her eyes, Emily saw the faces turn her way. Saw the hesitant smiles, heard the uncertain titters.

I won that round, didn't I? she wanted to crow. I shut him up fast!

But every time she opened her mouth to speak she broke out into a fresh spate of giggles. They rolled out of her mouth and across the patio like one of those Slinky toys she'd played with as a child, undulating up and down and around corners until the whole place was rocking with her merriment, and, try though she might, she couldn't stop it.

Lucas, though, didn't like being made a fool of. There was no missing his sudden scowl or the way he flung aside his napkin and shoved back his chair so abruptly that it fell backward and just about knocked a waiter off his feet.

That really set Emily off. She fairly screeched with laughter. Her grandmother wouldn't have approved at all. She didn't hold with ladies behaving like peasant washerwomen gathered around the village well. But then, Grand-mère wouldn't have approved of a Lamartine giving birth before she got married, either, so of the two the first was definitely the lesser sin.

"We're getting out of here," Lucas growled, throwing down a whole mess of money on the table.

Emily mopped her eyes with her napkin and hiccuped. "But I haven't finished my chowder," a whiny little voice that she recognized as hers protested.

He didn't care. Grasping her by the arm, he escorted her across the brick-tiled patio and out into the street with the dispatch of a sheriff marching a dangerous offender to the paddy wagon.

"You've got other things to finish," he said darkly, strong-arming her around the corner to where his car was parked under the shade of a tree. Wrenching open the front door, he shoveled her into the passenger seat, locked her in, then raced around to the driver's side.

"I have?" she gasped, between titters. "Like what?"

"Like explaining what the bloody hell you were hinting at, before you decided to put on a floor show for the whole restaurant," he snapped, climbing in behind the steering wheel.

Although he drove a station wagon, it wasn't a very big car. No more than a few inches and the gear shift separated her from him. If he'd wanted to, he could have closed both hands around her throat and strangled her without having to bestir himself very much at all. And, from the expression on his face, strangling her was just about what he had in mind.

All at once, things weren't so funny any more. The farce had played itself out and left her with the same old tragedy. The laughter dried up as suddenly as it had spurted forth. "Oh, dear!" she whispered, aghast at what she'd done.

"I'm waiting," Lucas said.

He looked formidable, his eyes blazing and the line of his mouth so sternly unyielding that she almost felt afraid of him. There was nothing left of that laughing, handsome youth she'd fallen in love with, nor even of the irresistibly aloof young man she'd so inexpertly seduced. This was a stranger bent on exacting a terrible price for what she'd done to him.

"Good gracious," she quavered, grasping at the only straw to present itself, "don't tell me you were taken in by my little joke?"

He moved then with the swiftness of a very lethal animal pouncing on its prey. His fingers closed again around her upper arm and yanked her around so that she was hauled half out of her seat and held so close to him that she could feel his breath winnowing over her face. "Spell it out, Emily Jane. I want to know about the rabbit."

"What rabbit? Did I mention a rabbit?" She raised her eyebrows and tried to look guileless. "Dear me, did the waiter perhaps spike the iced tea with vodka, do you think?"

He shook her then, a sharp little jolt that snapped her face up to meet his. "Tell me, you little witch, or so help me I'll...!"

She knew then that she'd spilled too much of the truth to back away from the rest, but she would not let him see how intimidated she was, nor would she tolerate his manhandling. Drawing on her shriveled courage, she attempted to stare him down. "Why, Lucas, I had no idea you hid such a violent streak under all that saintly professional politesse. Unhand me at once."

It was a wasted effort. He simply drew her so close that he could have kissed her had he felt so inclined. But acting the lover now was even farther from his mind than it had been eleven years earlier.

"If this is your idea of paying me back for that one time we were..." an expression of distaste flitted across his features as he searched for the right word to describe their lovemaking "...*together,* then you're going to have to come up with something more original than the old pregnancy number. Because if you'd had a baby the Lamartine outrage would have echoed clear around the world. And we both know, don't we, that not a whisper of any such scandal made itself heard?"

"Relax, Lucas; you're not a father," she said, fury and the mourning regret she'd never quite managed to leave behind rising up to choke her at the ease with which he disclaimed the child she'd conceived.

He went limp with relief and slackened his grip on her. "I didn't really think I was. But that was a dirty trick to play, Emily Jane. You really had me going for a while."

"I miscarried in my ninth week."

If vengeance had been her intent, she knew at once that she'd succeeded better than she could possibly have hoped. Her words hung in the air between them, as ominous as the blade of a guillotine suspended above the head of its victim.

Lucas's hand remained loosely shackled to her wrist and the only things that moved in the heavy silence were the pupils of his eyes, which widened in shock.

"You're not joking," he said at last, his voice cracking under the weight of reluctant certainty.

"No, I'm not," she said. "Despite my admittedly misleading exhibition back there in the restaurant, I do not now, nor have I ever found my miscarriage cause for amusement. I loved our baby and I have never recovered from losing him, nor ever quite forgiven you for ignoring the possibility that pregnancy might have occurred as a result of the night we were..." she curled her lip and tossed his scornful euphemism back at him "...together."

"*Forgive me?*" he echoed incredulously. "Let's run the movie through again, Emily Jane, because I seem to have missed something the first time around. What did I ever do or say that you took as encouragement to come sneaking into my bed?"

"I know you didn't invite me to fling myself at you, Lucas, but you didn't turn away from me, either, until after the damage was done."

"That hardly makes me the villain of the piece."

"I never said it did. The point is that I was, as you so painfully pointed out, nothing but a girl, and woefully ignorant of the possible consequences of what took place between us, whereas you were a doctor and had no such excuse. At the time, the way you simply walked away from the whole sorry incident and left me to cope on my own broke my heart. Now it merely incites my contempt."

"You knew enough to seduce me," he snarled. "I find it hard to believe you didn't also know that intercourse frequently leads to pregnancy."

"I was a virgin and I thought I was in love. The uglier realities didn't impress themselves on me until it was too late."

All the rage seemed to drain out of him at that, and a great sadness took its place. "Oh, *hell*, Emily!" he whispered, and his eyes had that shiny glaze to them that usually preceded tears.

Heaven help her, she wanted to comfort him—partly because she knew exactly the grief that tore at him, but also because she couldn't bear to see him so miserable. But she knew how he'd react to that—he'd turn away from her and shut her out. Again. And she'd had enough of his rejection to last her a lifetime.

So, she shrugged herself loose from his touch, checked the clock on the dashboard, and said briskly, "Now, having got that off my chest, I'd like to pick up my grandmother. It's well after two and she must be wondering what's keeping me."

For a moment he sat slumped over the steering wheel, then, without a word, slid the car into gear and made an illegal U turn in the middle of the road. Nothing was said during the five minutes it took for them to drive to the hospital and it was a silence fraught with unhappy tension.

Thoroughly unnerved, as soon as Lucas had parked Emily practically bolted out of the car in her eagerness to get away from him. That he would simply let the matter rest now that he'd wormed the truth out of her was, she supposed, expecting too much.

She supposed right.

He waited until she was halfway up the ramp leading to the double doors of the building, then he stuck his head out of the car window and bellowed after her, "In case you're wondering, this conversation isn't over by a long shot, so don't bother making any plans for later, Emily Jane. You and I will be taking a walk far enough away from the house that I can tell you, without fear of anyone overhearing, exactly what I think of the stunt you've just pulled."

She acknowledged the information with a defiant little toss of her head, but inside, where he couldn't see, her blood ran cold with foreboding. She had hoped that airing the truth would set her free but she'd been wrong. The past could be laid to rest only when Lucas, too, had made his peace with it. And that meant him probing at old wounds, ripping at scars it had taken her years to heal.

Pray heaven she could protect her heart better this time around.

He watched her sashay into the hospital, hips swaying, hair floating about her shoulders, carriage proud and defiant. If he hadn't witnessed it firsthand he'd never have believed that less than ten minutes before hysteria had torn her apart at the seams, and he was amazed at the speed with which she'd pulled herself together again.

The same couldn't be said for him. He was still reeling from her bombshell, but, over and above that, a slow-building mélange of emotions boiled within him. Fury, guilt, regret and something else—something that hinged too close to a truth he'd never allowed himself to acknowledge—swirled around, battering him no matter how he tried to turn away from them.

Things hadn't ended with his booting her out of his bed and out of his life. There'd been a child, *his* child, and he'd never known. About the time Emily Jane had miscarried, he'd been embarking on a future with Sydney, one which she'd persuaded him shouldn't include children.

"There are already so many poor little souls with no one to care for them," she'd said. "Let's make that our mission, darling. After all, we have so much to offer, and what's so special about giving birth? Cats and rabbits reproduce at the drop of a hat, but we don't award medals for it."

At the time, it had seemed a noble sacrifice for a couple afire with the sort of ideals and improbable zeal that only the very young and naive possessed. It was years later, when the disillusionment had soured him, before he'd come to question the rightness of their decision.

Nothing one man could do made the world a better place, and by the time he'd realized that his heart had been wrung as dry as the desert, its well of compassion and love long ago depleted. Might he not have found the energy to keep on giving if he'd had a child of his own, a personal investment in the future? And a woman who—?

No! Quickly, before it took hold and created even more upheaval than that which already existed, he closed his mind to the sheer futility of such a notion. It was too late by almost a dozen years to change history.

Frustrated, he slammed a fist against the dashboard. Whatever had made him think he could find peace here, where everything conspired to remind him of past mistakes? Why hadn't he shipped out the minute he'd discovered that Emily Jane had come back to haunt him? Because that was what she was doing—and had been for years, if truth be told. Looking back, he could see that his life had started to spin out of control from the very moment she'd tried to hitch her star to his.

Initially, he'd thought it was Sydney who'd climbed into bed with him that stifling August night. If he hadn't been sleeping so soundly, of course, he'd have known differently, but when a guy awoke to find long, silken limbs twined around his and a sweet, hot mouth making forays over his skin his first reaction was not to ask for ID—not unless he'd been neutered.

Sydney had wanted to wait until after they were married before they made love. "Over the long haul, marriage isn't about sex, darling," she'd said. "It's about commitment and the sharing of ideals. It's about friendship and trust."

So he'd known how her lips felt beneath his: firm and cool and closed. He'd known her scent: clean and fresh and slightly antiseptic. He'd known that if he caught her in a corner of the hospital and tried to steal a kiss she always kept one eye open in case someone should see them behaving unprofessionally.

Given all those things, he supposed he ought to have realized at once that it was completely out of character for her to wait until she was a guest in his grandmother's house and then steal into his room on her very first night to incite him to the sort of behavior she'd firmly refused to encourage when they'd been alone together in her apartment or his.

And if he'd been too stunned with delight to question such unusual audacity he bloody well should have known at once that there was no way on God's green earth that she would be such a tigress in bed. It just wasn't her style, as he'd discovered at married leisure.

He drummed his fingers on the rim of the steering wheel and scowled out at the sun-dappled scene before him, as if doing so would erase the outrageous memories chasing through his mind. Emily was right: he hadn't been blameless.

The moon had been huge that night, and as yellow as ripe old Cheddar. A harvest moon of gigantic proportions. It had cast a light as bright as day into his room, glazing everything it touched in soft gold: her hair, her throat, her lips.

He had woken to full arousal and the feel of her slipping down his torso an inch at a time. Torn between the pleasure of being seduced and the urgent demands of a body far more thoroughly awakened than the mind that should have been controlling it, he had allowed her to do as she pleased. And she had pleased him very much.

What experience had not taught her, instinct did. Generosity, tenderness, passion—she'd given them all. And he, selfish jerk that he'd been, had taken, sating himself at her expense. Only when his needs had been met had he addressed hers, and then not kindly.

"Emily Jane?" he whispered in frozen horror. "What the hell are you doing in my bed?"

"Loving you, Lucas," she said.

Just that. No excuses, no lies, no artifice.

"You can't," he said.

"I can't not," she replied, her voice filled with husky certainty. "I fell in love with you the first time you kissed me four years ago, and I couldn't wait any longer for you to tell me you feel the same way about me. Because I know you do, Lucas. I can tell from the way you look at me when you think no one's noticing, and from the way you've tried to avoid me ever since you came back this summer. That's why I came to you tonight—to let you know that you don't have to do that any more. I'm no longer a schoolgirl and it's all right for everyone to know we belong to each other."

He listened in stunned disbelief and felt the sweat break out down his spine. "No, Emily Jane, it isn't all right and we don't—*can't* belong to each other!"

She turned huge, limpid eyes his way and must have read the truth she saw in his because her lower lip trembled as she pleaded, "Why not? You do love me, don't you, Lucas?"

"Yes—*no!* Not like that!"

"But just now you—we...."

He sprang out of bed, belatedly and excruciatingly conscious that all the time they'd been debating the issue she'd been lying beneath him and they were both as naked as jaybirds.

"I thought...." He looked wildly around for something behind which to hide, as if covering up his nudity would erase the magnitude of what had occurred. Snatching up a pair of denim cut-offs, he climbed into them with record-breaking speed and searched for a way to extricate himself from a situation that was impossible for more reasons than she could begin to comprehend. "I thought I was dreaming."

She sat up then and let the sheet billow down around her hips, so that he could see how pretty her breasts were, and how narrow her waist. To his chagrin, desire flared within him again and this time there was no blaming it on sleep.

"It was real," she said.

He spun away from her and raked his fingers through his hair. "What's real," he replied, trying to bend truth to exonerate himself, "is that you're barely out of high school. All you've talked about, ever since I got here a week ago, is your coming-out ball, the parties you'll be attending, the trip to Europe that your parents are giving you for graduation. And I—"

She saw the direction his argument was taking and jumped in to deflect it. "I'll give them all up, Lucas. They don't matter. Nothing matters as long as we're together."

"You can't do that. What will your family say?"

"They'll understand. I'll make them understand."

Kindness hadn't worked. He'd had to be brutal. "No," he said, swinging back to confront her. "The point is, our interests—yours and mine, Emily Jane—are poles apart. You're a party girl and I'm a medical intern. The two don't mix and, even if they did, at your age you shouldn't have to give up the things that matter to you, especially not for a crush that you'll outgrow before the end of the month."

Of all the platitudes he'd spouted, it was that word "crush" that did it for her. She grew very still, her gaze fixed on him unblinkingly. And then, slowly and with painful dignity, she slipped out of his bed and into the clothes she'd dropped on the floor. He remembered them to this day: a pair of white shorts and a red and white striped vest top. No underpants, no bra, no shoes. She'd come prepared for action.

"I'll prove that there's more to it for me than that," she said quietly. "It doesn't matter how long it takes; I'll wait until you're ready to face up to the truth. You'll see, Lucas."

Then she left the room the same way she'd come in—via the tree growing outside his window. He watched her race off in the moonlight, her long, tanned legs carrying her out of sight in a matter of seconds.

At the time, he focused on the way she'd shimmied down the forked tree trunk, convinced that it validated everything he'd said to her. She *was* just a kid, too young to know where her life was headed, too young to understand the sort of life to which he was committed. She would soon forget him. And, bastard that he was, he had just the medicine on hand to speed things up.

The next evening, he gave Sydney the ring, and made their engagement official at the party Beatrice threw for them. The day after, he went over to Belvoir and introduced his fiancée.

He hadn't seen Emily Jane again until yesterday. That was not to say, however, that she hadn't continued to plague him one way or another.

Not once during his marriage had he experienced a repeat of the same sexual exhilaration he'd known that night with her. At first, he'd worried about it, had felt that it was up to the man to make things good for the woman and that somehow he was failing Sydney. But the bottom line was that his wife had found sex messy, and her habit of discussing patients during foreplay had been a real turn-off. Unjustly, perhaps, he'd blamed Emily for that, believing that her uninhibited pleasure in the act had left him with unrealistic expectations.

To discover now that she'd also denied him knowledge of their child ripped his guts apart. He could throttle her for what she'd done to him, and the fact that her list of sins just kept on growing merely fueled his rage.

* * *

The journey back to Roscommon was pure hell, as Emily had known it would be. Already annoyed at learning that she'd be confined to a wheelchair for the next week or so, and that she had little choice but to accept Beatrice's hospitality until Belvoir was habitable again, Monique was less than gracious at also being forced to accept the favor of having Lucas act as chauffeur.

"Why can't you rent a car, Emily Jane?" she'd demanded, when she'd found out. "Why do we have to rely on him?"

"Because there aren't any car rental agencies in April Water, Grand-mère. If I'd known you'd sold the Lincoln, I'd have arranged to pick up a car at the San Francisco airport. As it is, we don't have much choice but to take what's available."

Monique was barely settled in the back seat of the station wagon, with the wheelchair jammed into the luggage space behind her, before she started needling Lucas.

"You're driving much too fast," she complained, rapping him on the shoulder with the end of her cane. "I'm no more anxious to be landed back at Roscommon than you are to have me there, but that's not to say I consider death by highway misadventure a preferable alternative."

Emily saw Lucas's knuckles whiten around the steering wheel and the speedometer needle jump forward. "What did the doctor have to say after he'd examined you, Grand-mère?" she inquired hastily, aware that, in his present state of mind, it wouldn't take much to incense Lucas so thoroughly that he drove them all off the road.

"I am remarkable for a woman my age. I emerged from last night's mishap with nothing more than pulled ligaments in my knee." Monique preened briefly then drew a scornful breath. "Not that I set much store by anything he had to say, you understand. Doctors are all fools, some of them big enough that even *they* know they're useless and get out of the business before they kill *someone else*. Lucas Flynn, slow down this minute!''

"Grand-mère, please!" Emily sighed, feeling the beginnings of a headache that probably had been building since yesterday. "It's been a tough enough day without your making it worse."

"And whose fault is that?" Monique demanded, glaring at the back of Lucas's neck.

"Mine," he said obligingly, then reached forward and turned on the radio full blast.

It proved an effective deterrent to further conversation.

When they arrived at Roscommon, they found Beatrice entertaining a visitor, a tall, good-looking man somewhere in his mid-thirties, with slightly thinning dark blond hair. He was almost as tanned as Lucas and that, coupled with his strong, athletic build, suggested an active, outdoor lifestyle.

Beatrice made the introductions. "Monique, Emily Jane, this is Mr. Anderson. He's staying with the Barretts just now. This is Madame Lamartine, Mr. Anderson, and her granddaughter, Emily Jane."

"How do you do?" he said, striding forward to help Monique into the wheelchair which Lucas had just hauled in from the car. "We met last night but you had other things on your mind at the time and I don't expect you to remember. I stopped by to see how you were feeling and to apologize for not having called earlier."

"We owe our lives to you, young man," Monique declared, visibly placated by his good manners, "and quite possibly our home."

He smiled, displaying enviably perfect teeth, and accepted the handshake she offered. "It was my pleasure, ma'am. I'm sorry I couldn't have done more."

Emily was quite bowled over by the smile. It was such a nice change from the scowls to which Lucas had treated her for most of the day. "How do we begin to thank you, Mr. Anderson?"

"You can start by calling me Bruce, and allow me to take you to dinner some time soon."

"That hardly seems fair. We're the ones in *your* debt."

He shrugged disarmingly. "Then you can make dinner for me. I never turn down the chance of a home-cooked meal."

"She won't feel comfortable doing that while she's living in my house, what with her having to keep an eye on her granny and all," Beatrice piped up. "But I'm more than happy to offer an invitation. I've got a lovely chicken roasting in the oven. Come back and join us tonight around half past six, why don't you?"

"I wouldn't dream of it on such short notice, Mrs. Flynn, but I do thank you for asking." He turned to Emily and took her hand. "I'll call again soon, if I may?"

Beatrice, however, wasn't finished. "I won't take no for an answer," she insisted. "Emily Jane, convince this young man that we'd enjoy his company."

Aware of Lucas skulking in the background, Emily left her hand wrapped in Bruce's firm clasp and returned his smile. "It really would be our pleasure."

He capitulated with a good-natured shrug. "Very well, then; if you're sure I'm not imposing, I accept. Thank you."

Emily strolled with him to the front door and when he seemed disinclined to leave right away lingered with him on the porch. In the deep shade cast by the eaves hung the old glider which Beatrice's husband had built for her when her children were small. Sinking onto its deep cushions with a sigh of relief, Emily lightly massaged her temples.

Bruce regarded her intently for a moment then dropped down beside her and set the glider in motion. "Headache?" he inquired sympathetically.

"A little." She closed her eyes briefly, annoyed that she couldn't control her emotions better. "Things are a little...tense around here, and I don't seem to be coping very well.''

He dipped his head in apology. ''Forgive me if I asked out of turn. It's an occupational habit that's hard to break.''

''How so?''

''I'm a police officer when I'm not on holiday. Interrogation comes with the territory.''

''I'd never have guessed!'' she exclaimed, genuinely surprised. ''You don't look the type to be hauling hardened criminals in off the streets.''

''Most of the time I'm not. I'm with the Royal Canadian Mounted Police and currently stationed in a small community north of the border in Ontario. We don't see much big city crime up there.''

Emily stared at him in frank delight. ''You mean I'm talking to a real live Mountie?''

''Afraid so.''

''Heavens, don't apologize! I have a niece who's addicted to a TV show starring one of your types and she'll never forgive me if I let you escape without getting your autograph.''

He actually blushed. ''Well, that'll make a nice change from some of the things I've been invited to do.'' He hesitated a moment as though weighing his next words, then said, ''Will you walk a little way down the drive with me, Emily?''

She nodded her assent and, when he drew her up out of the glider and offered his arm, slipped her hand in the crook of his elbow. It seemed such an easy, natural thing to do, with none of that stabbing electricity that punctuated any sort of physical contact with Lucas. ''How long do you expect to stay in California, Bruce?''

''About a month. And you?''

''Initially I'd planned on only a week or two, but now, with things the way they are, it looks as though it's going to turn into a more permanent arrangement. Not that I really mind. I've always liked northern California."

"I can't say I'm sorry either. We might be able to stretch that dinner date to two."

He was so nice. So big and solid and dependable. So flatteringly attentive. "What a very pleasant thing to look forward to," she said.

Lucas was lurking at the foot of the stairs when she returned to the house. "Did Prince Valiant finally ride off into the sunset?"

"Mr. Anderson has left, if that's what you mean, though why you should care is beyond me."

"I don't care," he rushed to inform her.

Of course he didn't. He never had. "Then why are you hanging around here waiting to ambush me when we both have better things to do?"

"Because you and I have a date that takes precedence over anything your red-jacketed Mountie might have proposed."

"How do you know he's a Mountie?" she asked sharply.

"I overheard him tell you so during your little tête à tête on the porch."

Inexplicably, the admission warmed her heart, perhaps because, although his expression remained neutral enough, his voice betrayed an edge that smacked of jealousy. "That's called eavesdropping, Lucas," she declared smugly.

"Never mind trying to change the subject," he snapped. "We'd planned on going for a walk together, remember?"

He didn't sound jealous any longer; he sounded thoroughly ticked off, as though having to deal with someone like her was more than should be expected of any man.

"Oh, I think not," she said. "I see no point in dragging up ancient history, particularly since nothing either of us can say will change the facts."

"It isn't ancient history for me, Emily Jane, it's news that I haven't fully digested. And I intend to get to the bottom of every last, miserable detail before I file them away in my memory bank."

She supposed that, in his place, she'd feel the same way. But, what with jet lag and everything that had happened in the last twenty-four hours, she simply wasn't up to another go-round with him. "Not today, Lucas. I've got a headache."

"Then I suggest you take two aspirin with water before we go out. That and the fresh air will do you a world of good."

Was it marriage that had turned him into such a pedantic boor or had he always been like that and she too much the moonstruck teenager to notice? she wondered.

"You're not my doctor," she snapped, scooting past him. "From what I understand, you're not *anybody's* doctor any more, so keep your medical opinions to yourself."

All the way up the stairs she felt his eyes raking over her, full of scorn and resentment, yet she had no one to blame but herself. She'd had to spill out her feelings, exactly as she had the night she'd stolen into his bed. And, just as she had then, she'd left herself at his unkind mercy.

By the time she reached her room and lowered the shades over the windows, her head really was throbbing. How had a perfectly simple visit to her grandmother's so quickly turned into such a convoluted mess?

She stayed upstairs for the rest of the afternoon and even managed to sleep a little. Just before six, she took a shower then changed into one of the outfits she'd brought over from Belvoir, a plain cotton skirt and an embroidered white blouse.

When she came downstairs, she found that Bruce had already arrived and everyone was gathered at the back of the house, in the sun room that overlooked the river. The old ladies were bickering in a bid to secure Bruce's attention, but amiably for a change, probably because they'd both been at the sherry. Lucas stood apart from them, gazing moodily out at the view and nursing a glass half-full of something dark and evil-looking.

Monique interrupted her discourse on the finer points of juvenile crime prevention to ask, "Are you feeling a little better, Emily Jane? Lucas Flynn told us you 'claimed' to have a headache—a fact which, given the circumstances, hardly struck me as surprising but which he seemed to find quite preposterous."

"Thank you, yes, I'm feeling much better." Emily smiled a greeting at Bruce and bent to kiss her grandmother's cheek. "How about you, Grand-mère? Is the knee very painful?"

"Not as long as I keep off it, which this contraption allows me to do. It's fortunate, also, that Mrs. Flynn happens to have a bedroom on the main floor which enables me to rest whenever I feel the need."

"And there's nothing like a nap in the afternoon to restore a body—even one as old as yours, Monique," Beatrice observed with tipsy relish. "Lucas, you're not being a very good host. Will you pour a drink for Emily Jane?"

"What would you like?" He wasn't so much truculent as indifferent. Bestirring himself from the scowling perusal of his own libation, he tossed the question at Emily with such a marked lack of interest in her reply that she felt sure if she'd asked for belladonna extract on the rocks it wouldn't have caused him a moment's disquiet.

Sheer mischief prompted her to indicate the glass Bruce held and say, "I'll have one of those."

"Beer?" Lucas snorted, successfully shaken out of his black reverie.

Only he could have bathed so harmless a word with such sarcasm. "Is there something wrong with beer?" she inquired sweetly.

"I'd have thought champagne cocktails were more your style."

"You don't know enough about me to leap to any such conclusion, Lucas," she said, at which her grandmother let out an unladylike cackle of approval and took another snort of sherry.

He glowered impressively and muttered, "I know a hell of a lot more than I did yesterday at this time."

It wasn't so much what he said as the unspoken implication that, before he'd done, he'd put her entire life for the last eleven years under a microscope and examine it in minute detail. It was a prospect which, to her disgust, Emily found strangely exhilarating, and which left the atmosphere humming with danger.

Was she really still so foolish as to believe that any sort of notice from him was better than none?

Rattled, she swung away from him and turned her attention to Bruce. He was the ideal guest—urbane, witty, congenial—everything, indeed, that Lucas was not. But not even his presence was quite enough to diffuse her morbid sense of expectation every time Lucas cast an ominous glance in her direction.

When Bruce suggested a stroll by the river after dinner, she leapt at the chance to postpone the confrontation that she knew was brewing.

When she returned, shortly before eleven, the house was in darkness and she breathed a sigh of relief. Of course, sooner or later she and Lucas would have things out, but far better that it be later. Hopefully, by then she'd have overcome the insane urge to forget all the reasons she had for disliking him.

She took off her sandals and stole up the stairs, her bare feet making not a sound on the thick carpet. Apart from a night lamp burning on the landing, not a crack of light showed anywhere.

Noiselessly she traversed the upper hall, and let the door to her room snick closed behind her. And knew at once that she'd gained no advantage at all.

The beat of his heart pulled her like a magnet. The force of his personality coiled across the room, tugging her forward in the darkness until he could, had he chosen, have reached out and touched her.

Far from eluding him, she had walked blithely into a trap the irony of which only he and she could possibly have appreciated. He had come sneaking into her room while her back was turned and was stretched out on her bed, waiting for her.

It was déjà vu with a difference. Because this time *he* was the one to invade *her* privacy, and, from the look on his face when he flicked on the bedside light, she had the distinct feeling she wasn't going to find the action quite as pleasurable as she had when she'd been the one to initiate things.

CHAPTER FIVE

"WELL, well," he drawled, "here you are at last, all flushed and breathless. Do I take that to mean he got more than just a goodnight kiss?"

Had it been anyone—*anyone*—but Lucas, she'd have reacted like the morally outraged woman she was and pinned his ears so far back that they met behind his head. But it wasn't someone else; it was the man who'd hurt her more than any other person she'd ever known by dismissing her love as adolescent delusion, and who'd then added insult to injury by making her feel cheap and foolish into the bargain.

The fact that he was still doing it, without provocation this time, and with that affectation of nonchalant contempt that seemed to be his stock-in-trade these days, inspired her to respond in kind. So instead of freezing him with icy disdain she swept her hair away from her face in a deliberately sultry gesture and replied, "Don't worry, Lucas. I've grown smart enough over the years not to run the risk of getting pregnant."

He spiraled off the bed so fast, he was nothing but a blur of movement. "How do you stand yourself?" he snarled, looming over her. "How do you look at yourself in the mirror every morning and not throw up?"

"I manage," she said, standing her ground even though every instinct of self-preservation told her to back down.

For several charged seconds he was transformed. His eyes glowed with angry blue fire, his chest heaved, his hands curled into fists. He became again that man she used to know, passionate about life and death and all

73

the bits, good or bad, in between. The miracle of it washed over her and cleansed away all the grime that was part and parcel of the adult world, and for a very little while she remembered why, a long time ago, she had fallen in love with him.

And then he seemed to remember who she was and that he didn't care what she did or with whom as long as it didn't involve him. She saw the emotion seep out of him and the familiar shroud of indifference drape his features. The flame in his eyes died, leaving them flat and opaque. His mouth, which once had kissed her with such hunger, narrowed in censure. His face became that of an avenging angel confronted by the most reprehensible sinner to crawl the earth, and she couldn't stand it.

"Don't look at me as if I'm nothing," she cried.

"You're less than nothing," he said coldly. "I don't know how your husband abides you."

She gave a croak of laughter. "He doesn't. He left me nearly two years ago because—"

"So that's why you still call yourself Lamartine—not that I'm interested in hearing the sordid details."

"I couldn't give him a child, so he turned to a woman who could."

Why hadn't she heeded his admonition? What demon of perversity had driven her to prick his bubble of containment and try to squeeze another drop of human emotion out of him when his every word and gesture told her that he had none to spare? An urge to revive the life that had gone out of his soul, perhaps—or the need to punish him? Whatever the motive, her perseverance backfired, buffeting her with regrets that raged at the old wounds and set them bleeding again.

She saw his spine stiffen, saw the stillness drop over him like a cloak. "Couldn't give him a child—or wouldn't?"

"Couldn't, though heaven knows I tried."

His gaze scoured her face, seeking out evidence of lies, of games, of pretence, and finding none. "I'm sorry."

"So am I," she said, on a quiet sigh of distress. "So am I. I would have liked children."

He lifted his hand in sympathy. Almost touched her arm, in a kindly, doctorish sort of way. "It's possible you could still have them. We've come a long way in the treatment of infertility. Have you seen a specialist?"

Blinking, she turned away and tried for a lighter note. "No. I think I'd prefer to have a husband first."

"You're planning to remarry, then?"

"No, but nor am I interested in becoming a single parent. I don't have the sort of courage that inspired me when I was nineteen."

The door on the big wardrobe was covered with a full-length mirror. In its reflection she saw the different expressions chasing across his face—the anger softened by compassion, the curiosity vying with regret.

"If you had carried my child to term," he finally asked in a low voice, "would you have told me?"

She shook her head and pretended an interest in the cuticle of her right forefinger. "You were in love with Sydney. By the time I realized there was a baby on the way, you'd set a wedding date. I took that as a pretty clear signal that you'd meant what you said the night you threw me out of your room, and that we had no future together."

"Whom did you tell?"

Whom, he'd said. So unimpeachably, grammatically correct, as if that would mitigate the impropriety of their sexual encounter!

"No one. Initially, I was too afraid—of the disgrace, of my parents' disappointment and shame."

"You mean you went through it all alone? Couldn't you have confided in a friend?"

Again, she shook her head, though she dared not risk looking at him. Her feelings were too close to the surface, too disturbing. "My friends were occupied with other things. Their lives revolved around what to wear, who—*whom* to date, college, travel, cars, and suddenly I was no longer a member of the club. I had other cares, other concerns, and didn't belong. I felt alone and..." she lifted her shoulders in an unhappy shrug as the memory of that time replayed itself in her mind's eye "...I felt *old*. Yet I was still just a girl, barely out of school, with none of the wisdom or maturity that comes with age.

"And then, suddenly, it didn't matter any more. It was all over, with no one any the wiser—except for me and the night staff in the emergency ward at our local hospital."

"You said this morning that you miscarried. Did you...do something—?"

She swung back to face him, appalled. "No! I was unhappy and confused about a lot of things, but I never wanted to lose my baby. You had given it to me. It was all I had left of you."

This time, he was the one to turn away, flinging a resentful glance over his shoulder as he did so. "Stop that!"

"What?"

"Talking as if we were lovers and I betrayed you."

"You might not like hearing this, but I did love you, Lucas, for a very long time. I think that was another reason why my marriage failed. In the deepest sense, I was unfaithful to my husband from the very start."

"No." He spun back toward her, anguish blazing in his face. *"No!"*

She took a step closer to him. "Why are you so afraid of the truth, Lucas? You never used to be such a coward."

"It isn't truth, it's fantasy—*your* fantasy."

"If you really believe that, why are you so upset?" She moved closer and laid her hand softly against his jaw, empathy welling within her at the misery imprinted on his face. "What's happened to you that you prefer to exist in a vacuum rather than face life head-on, the way you used to? Why do you try to look through me, instead of at me? Or pretend that nothing touches you any more?"

He took her hand between his thumb and two fingers and held it away from him as if it were a particularly repugnant insect. "I'm not the man I used to be, Emily," he said flatly, "and I was never the man you chose to believe I was."

Quite what prompted her next action was unclear. Perhaps it was the underlying sadness she saw in him that moved her to compassion, or perhaps it was the old magic at work again, brought back by the touch of his flesh on hers.

Whatever, spontaneously, without forethought or foresight, she dipped her head and pressed her lips to the inside of his wrist, right at the spot where his pulse throbbed.

"You were good and kind and brave, and all I ever wanted," she said, the sincerity of her words vibrating against his smooth, tanned skin. "And somewhere, deep down, that man still exists."

A lighted match thrown into a can of gasoline couldn't have ignited any faster. The cadence of his blood altered, accelerating wildly. He uttered a harsh gasp as though racked by a pain too fierce to be borne.

And then he was holding her crushed against him, and his mouth was on hers, but it wasn't déjà vu any more, because she was no longer a girl, unsure of the message she was receiving; she was a woman who knew very well when a man was in torment.

His kiss was fired with desperation, torn out of him against his better judgement, and yet he was starving, dying, for want of a woman's healing touch. It showed in the way his lips hungered over hers and returned to

them, time and again, despite his best efforts to put an
end to the encounter.

It showed, too, in the stirring response of his body,
in the way his hand slipped down to her lower back and
pressed her against him, inch for aroused inch.

But not in his eyes. Those he closed so that their
message would remain unread. It was the last thing she
saw before her own followed suit, albeit for different
reasons.

How quickly they all rushed back: the sweeping, tur-
bulent ache of desire, the fiery passion, the lyrical
sweetness of a love no less potent for its long hiber-
nation. Emily felt herself slipping under their spell again,
swirling to another dimension which did not acknowledge old hurts and disappointments but which
beckoned with the promise of new beginnings and different, better endings.

He felt it, too. She could tell by the way his groan of
despair quieted to a sigh as their mouths bonded, the
separate parts merging into a sensuous ballet of motion.
His lips opened against hers, his tongue tasted, flirted,
begged, and sent its erotic message speeding through her
blood. Sensation quivered low in her womb, a cloud of
desire so swollen with expectation that it quickly dissolved into a shower of heat between her thighs.

He stole her breath away, along with all her fine resolve to resist him, to hate him. Slowly, she sank to the
bed and drew him down beside her, her mouth still fused
with his. Looping one hand around his neck, she let the
other slide inside his shirt and over the lovely, taut planes
of his chest.

She found his heart and pressed her palm there,
wishing she could capture his love as easily. She roamed
the smooth skin of his ribs, the indentation that marked
his waist, and then, driven by mindless, voracious
hunger, she slipped her hand lower still, to the unmis-

takable swell of his erection beneath the rough fabric of his jeans.

She shouldn't have. Not if she wanted to prolong the dizzying pleasure. Not if she wanted more than merely to touch. Not if she wanted what she'd secretly missed for years: the feel of him buried deep inside her. And she did. She'd craved it from the moment she'd heard his name mentioned again.

But she didn't get it. Instead, he tore his mouth from hers and shoved her away. Unkindly, ungently. "Damn you!" he exploded, surging to his feet.

She stared up at him through dazed, passion-clouded eyes, disappointment aching within her. "Lucas, please!" she all but whimpered.

His gaze seared the length of her, blazing a trail of contempt from the curve of her throat, past the arch of her breasts to her thighs, which were parted and half-exposed where her skirt had ridden up. And yet she shivered in its aftermath, and felt numb, as if she were encased in ice.

"Please what?" he inquired with savage menace.

All manner of responses sprang to mind. Please don't despise me! Please don't leave me! Please love me, at least a little bit, just for tonight!

At nineteen, she might have uttered any one of them, then quietly bled as he rejected them all. At thirty, praise heaven, she was much less inclined to offer herself as a sacrifice on any man's altar. Drawing belated pride to her rescue, she reached down and restored a modicum of decency to her clothing. "Please leave," she said, bathing her bruised heart in the doubtful balm of this time being the one to evict him. "And please don't invite yourself back again."

Something was going to have to change. He'd thought so last night when he'd reeled out of her room and collapsed against the wall outside her door with his heart thudding like a thoroughbred's after a steeplechase. He'd reaffirmed the belief several times in the small hours between midnight and dawn, when that sly abductor, sleep, had lurked, waiting to shanghai him into some erotic dream-state over which *she* presided. And nothing about the new day held hope of any improvement—a fact he recognized with irritated resignation before he'd had time to warm the seat of his chair at the breakfast table.

"Emily Jane, darling, surely that's not all you're taking?" Beatrice exclaimed, pausing in the act of filling his coffee-cup to cast a scandalized glance at the slice of melon adorning Emily's plate. "How do you expect to get through the day if you don't properly stoke up your engine?"

"I never eat breakfast," Emily said, angling one shoulder just enough to preclude having to acknowledge his presence, which was fine by him. He wasn't particularly comfortable meeting her eye, either.

"Shame on you!" Beatrice scolded, clearly impervious to the tension which, in his view, was thick enough to cut with a knife. "Lucas, take a look at the girl. She's skinny as a rail and needs a qualified man like yourself to tell her so."

He shrugged and said, "She's a woman, not a girl, Bea, and old enough to decide for herself. If she's determined to go to hell in a hand cart, I doubt anything you or I have to say will change her mind."

"But you can try," his grandmother insisted. "She might listen, what with you being a doctor and all."

"No, I won't," Emily said flatly, addressing the space behind his left ear.

"Indeed not," her grandmother chipped in. "Trust me, Beatrice Flynn, there's nothing your grandson can offer my granddaughter that she'd be willing to accept."

She flushed then, a dusky rose that reminded him of sun-ripened peaches, and her glance flicked to his face before fleeing again to the refuge of the wall behind him.

Just briefly he was tempted to observe, I don't know about that. She seemed more than willing to take anything she could get her hands on last night, whether I offered it or not. Except that, for all his faults—and he'd be the first to admit he had plenty—he wasn't prepared to sink quite that far.

Especially since, damn it, his response to her hadn't been exactly indifferent, as she'd made a point of discovering for herself. So pretending his sole expenditure of energy had been in fending her off would have been a barefaced lie as well as boorish.

Amazingly, his grandmother still seemed unaware of the undercurrents. "Well, and why ever not, when the pair of them grew up like brother and sister? The way you talk, Monique Lamartine, you'd think our grandchildren were sworn enemies, when it's plain to see there's never been a cross word between them."

"Things aren't always as they seem," old lady Lamartine replied snidely, leaving Lucas to wonder just how much she knew of the true state of affairs.

He fixed his gaze first on her and then on Emily. "No, they're not," he said. "Isn't it nice that we finally agree on something, Mrs. Lamartine?"

Emily Jane came close to aspirating on her melon at that. Disappearing behind her serviette, she choked quietly and, when she'd recovered, muttered, "It's a lovely morning so, if you'll all excuse me, I'll take my coffee out to the porch and enjoy the sun."

Old habits died hard. "Wear a hat," he said automatically. "The sun's a lot stronger out here in the valley than what you've become accustomed to in Boston."

He should have kept his opinion to himself—and would have, if he'd known the reaction he'd provoke. Mrs. Lamartine sniffed as though to imply that she'd be inclined to consult a gypsy fortune teller before she'd listen to his advice. Emily Jane flung him a glance that suggested he could stuff his phoney concérn precisely where the sun didn't shine. And Beatrice, ever the optimist, beamed with delight. "Once a doctor—" she began.

He shoved back his chair. "Don't start on that old theme again, Bea," he snapped, venting his collective annoyance on her. "Even someone with a brain the size of a pea knows overexposure to sunlight is asking for trouble."

"That must explain why you're sporting such a spectacular tan," Emily Jane remarked sweetly, just before she let the door swing closed behind her.

He glowered into his coffee and wished he'd chosen a monastery in a remote corner of Tibet in which to seek out the peace and quiet his soul craved, because it became more apparent with every passing hour that he wasn't going to find them here.

Just to add insult to injury, Bruce Anderson showed up about half past eleven that morning—"to say hello and see how Emily and Madame Lamartine are feeling", if he was to be believed, but the alacrity with which he accepted Beatrice's invitation to join them for lunch on the patio left Lucas with the feeling that the visit had been timed with the hope of just such an offer being extended.

It wasn't that Lucas had anything against the guy—apart from his horse-sized teeth and a great honking laugh that resembled the mating call of a randy gander. In fact, under any other circumstances, he'd have been grateful to have another man around. Not only did it even the sides a little, it also provided the ladies with another victim on whom to shower attention—something they all seemed more than eager to do.

During the first course of the meal Lucas basked in the luxury of being ignored, but, by the time hot chicken salad replaced the chilled watercress soup, he showed all the symptoms of the onset of serious neglect. And it galled him more than he cared to admit that, with the appearance of raspberries in lavender cream, he felt about as imperative to the success of the party as an outbreak of cholera.

Conversation swirled over and around him as if he were a chunk of rock lodged in the middle of the river, a bit of an obstacle but not serious enough to interrupt the flow of things. If he'd keeled over face first into his plate, it was doubtful anyone would have noticed, he thought sourly.

The final straw came when the first bottle of wine ran dry. Before Lucas could open his mouth and offer to open another, good old Bruce the Canada Goose was on his feet and flourishing the corkscrew. "Allow me," he insisted.

Emily Jane regarded him as if he'd just come up with a cure for cancer. "It's wonderful to be around a man who's not afraid to take charge," she purred, batting eyelashes so absurdly long and thick that, if Lucas hadn't known for a fact otherwise, he'd have sworn they had to be artificial.

She and Anderson traded smiles then. That was all. But to Lucas on the sidelines, it was—absurdly, illogically—like finding himself cast in the role of the husband whose wife was conducting an affair right under his nose. He knew a savage desire to shove the Canadian's teeth down his throat, smash his nose until it cracked, and then boot the man into the river.

It took more control than he'd known he possessed to maintain a facade of indifference. To nod his thanks when his glass was topped up. To keep his hands loose and relaxed on the glass tabletop, instead of clenched in fury.

He succeeded by envisioning the majesty of the Himalayas on a far horizon, the pale silhouette of saffron robes against azure skies, the chime of temple bells echoing across the high plateaus of Tibet.

As an escape hatch they had never seemed more appealing. Trouble was, even he knew that the search for peace began not on a map of Asia but in a man's heart. And right now his was a battleground.

Lunch passed into early afternoon with no visible break in continuity. The sun arched overhead, tempered by the shade of the table umbrella. White geraniums and heliotrope nestled at the foot of potted scarlet hibiscus trees scattered around the perimeter of the patio, and clustered around the roots of the royal purple bougainvillaea climbing the south wall of the house.

The grandmothers dozed discreetly over their iced coffee. Bruce sprawled in his chair with his long legs stretched in front of him, seeming content to enjoy the drowsy silence.

If only Lucas hadn't been there, Emily might have relaxed. But there he was, a brooding presence she found impossible to ignore, his blue eyes hooded as they stared out at the river, his mouth paralleling the lean, severe angle of his jaw.

He wore chinos, clean but old, their fabric, like that of his white T-shirt, reduced to caressing softness by many launderings. It wasn't fair that they should outshine Bruce's starched and ironed elegance. It wasn't fair that, of the two good-looking men flanking her, it was Bruce's pleasant, open face she found forgettable, while the surly beauty of Lucas's features was etched for ever in her mind.

It was supremely unjust that her heart continued its even, unhurried rhythm when Bruce laid a hand on her bare arm and pointed out the hummingbirds darting around the flower pots, but that Lucas could send her into a tailspin simply by accidentally brushing the sole of his running shoe against her ankle as he shifted to a more comfortable position.

The sound of footsteps approaching along the brick-paved path at the side of the house, followed shortly thereafter by the appearance of a woman of about thirty-five, provided a welcome distraction.

"Hello!" Shading her eyes from the sun with her hand, the newcomer hesitated at the edge of the patio. "Sorry to intrude on a family gathering, but the clean-up crew next door told me that I'd find the person I'm looking for over here."

Her voice, charmingly husky and rich, brought the old ladies fully awake. Her legs—long, tanned and un-questionably gorgeous—had both men practically falling out of their chairs.

"Which person is that?" Lucas inquired, the cool, distant look in his eyes replaced by acute interest.

"The one who rushed to the rescue when the fire broke out the other night." She fished in the bag hanging from her shoulder and produced a card. "I'm Tamara Golding, PR manager at the April Valley Winery. When a real live hero pops up in our community, we like to acknowledge the fact."

"Then I'm the person you should be talking to," Monique informed her. "I discovered the fire."

"But the *real* heroes," Beatrice hastened to add, "are my grandson, Lucas Flynn, and Mr. Anderson, who happens to be visiting the area. *They* saved the house *and* the inhabitants."

"Really?" Ms. Golding's smile embraced them all but lingered longest on the men. "How fortuitous to find both stars in the same place at the same time. Any chance we could have a talk right now, or would you prefer I make an appointment?"

Her name fit her to a T. She was all golden skin and hair and sunny dimples. Her lemon cotton shift floated over her curves like a whisper and her strappy yellow sandals revealed elegant, narrow feet, their toenails glossed in shiny bronze polish that matched her fingertips.

Lucas outmaneuvered Bruce in pulling forward an extra chair for her. "I'm happy enough to accommodate you now."

Talk about overstating the obvious! He was practically drooling. So, for that matter, was Bruce. And Tamara Golding was doing her part by cosying up to them as if they were the first men to walk on the moon. Clearly, a mutual admiration group was about to host its inaugural meeting, and Emily wasn't sure she could watch and not lose her lunch. "Would you like me to make more iced coffee, Mrs. Flynn?"

"That would be lovely, darling. And there's fresh pound cake cooling on the kitchen table. Slice it up and pour over some of the mulberry syrup you'll find in the refrigerator."

In her line of work, Emily was on comfortable territory in anybody's kitchen, especially one as large and well equipped as the Flynns'. Add to that the fact that it was blessedly cool and quiet inside the house and she fully expected that the sudden, uncharacteristic jealousy she'd experienced at Tamara Golding's appearance would melt away.

She busied herself measuring beans into the grinder, filling the water reservoir on the automatic coffee-maker, scooping ice cream into a large glass pitcher, and waited for the calming routine to take effect.

It didn't happen. Her blood churned in time with the coffee-grinder at the thought of what she might be missing by isolating herself inside and leaving a clear field for Tamara, who no doubt was displaying her gorgeous legs to full advantage and further captivating her already willing audience.

Why was it, Emily wondered miserably, wielding a knife on the pound cake with deadly efficiency, that she was the only woman Lucas found so thoroughly resistible? Worse, when had she developed such a mean-spirited streak that she was prepared to dislike on sight a woman who'd done nothing to deserve her enmity? Because, she acknowledged as she sliced away at the cake, she would have been just as happy to hack off every last sleek hair from Tamara Golding's beautiful blond head.

She wasn't aware that Lucas had come into the kitchen until he spoke. "Is it pound cake in particular that you dislike, or do you mutilate all food like that?" He stood so close that the words practically kissed the back of her neck.

She whirled around, the knife still clutched in her hand, and found him regarding her with amused indulgence. As if she were a child who needed to be humored. As if she were a half-wit. Which she undoubtedly must be to be so thoroughly disconcerted by his proximity.

Praying for the wit to crush him with a truly brilliant retort, she muttered, "What are you doing here, Lucas?"

"Dear," he said kindly, "I live here."

"I know that. What I mean is, what are you doing in here, now, when we both know you'd rather be out there?" She flourished the knife disdainfully toward the door behind him.

"Be careful where you wave that thing, Emily Jane," he warned, backing away, "unless you want to end up slicing off more than you bargained for."

Oh, the replies that occurred to her! The truly sinful images that filled her mind! Reining in her imagination, she slammed the knife on the counter and, in the best tradition of Done To Perfection, poured elegant swirls of mulberry sauce over slivers of pound cake on delicate china dessert plates.

"Why don't you go back outside and talk to Tamara?" she spat, investing the last three words with such a world of petulance that he'd have had to be brain-damaged not to hear it.

And of course, being Lucas, he couldn't pass up the chance to display himself in a vastly more favorable light. "Because I thought you might need a hand in here." His beautiful blue eyes smiled down at her, and just about broke her heart. "But if that offends you I'll make myself scarce."

If only he had, before she'd come back to April Water! If only he'd stayed in Africa, half a world and a whole lifetime away! "Here," she muttered, closing her mind to such pointless, after-the-fact regrets as firmly as she knew how and sliding a tray loaded with tall crystal glasses down the counter toward him. "If you really want to make yourself useful, carry these outside."

"OK." He anchored the tray with one hand and watched her thoughtfully for a moment. "If you're worried that Tamara's horning in on your territory, don't be. Bruce only has eyes for you."

But she didn't care about what Bruce might be up to or with whom. In fact, all of a sudden and completely out of nowhere, she didn't care about anything. She felt empty and used up, even more than she had after she'd lost the baby. Because in the last two days she'd lost something else that she hadn't even known she possessed until it was stripped away, and that was the buried hope that perhaps, one day, all her adolescent dreams would come true.

How often, in the years immediately following her miscarriage, had she fortified herself with scenarios fed solely by wishful thinking and a heart starved for a taste of the sort of passion she'd only ever found with Lucas Flynn? Imagined that some day she'd walk down a street in Boston and bump into a stranger, and it would be Lucas, tall, dark and handsome still, but sadder and wiser for having almost lost her. And he would hold her hands and gaze down at her and say, "Emily, I've found you again!"

Or she'd look in her mailbox to discover an envelope plastered with foreign stamps, and inside a letter from him in which he'd tell her he'd made a mistake in walking away from her and ask if it was too late for them to start over.

How many times had she choreographed an affair for Boston's upper crust and thought that she'd spotted Lucas's height and breadth of shoulder among the distinguished guests, only to have the man in question turn around and reveal himself to be just another mortal, less than Lucas in every way?

It hadn't been rational and it hadn't been smart. Instead, it had been the sort of simplistic fantasy that old romantic movies were based on, where all the hurts and failures had a point to them because happy endings were supposed to come with a high price.

Real life was different, however, and she'd eventually accepted that she wasn't going to find any sort of happy ending with George. But that little fragment of hope had refused to die, so she'd wrapped up her fantasies about Lucas and put them into storage, just in case, some day....

Well, some day was now and Lucas had come crashing back into her life and shown up all that gauzy self-delusion for the nonsense it really was. Tomorrow wasn't going to be any better than today, and might conceivably be very much worse.

Small wonder he found her resistible! She was pathetic and it was long past time for her to reinvent herself.

"Emily Jane?"

She blinked, surprised to find him back in the kitchen and regarding her curiously. "Sorry. Did you say something?"

"What's keeping you? The others are waiting for you to come back out and join the party."

The others, perhaps, but not him. Never him!

"Tell them not to bother," she retorted, past caring
that she sounded like a sulky adolescent whose nose was
out of joint because things weren't going exactly her way.

Of course, he picked up on the fact. His perceptions
were amazingly acute when it came to pinpointing her
character flaws. "Now what's eating you, Emily Jane?
Or would I be better off not knowing?"

"I have to phone the airline and make a reservation,"
she said rashly.

"Why?"

"Because I'm planning to travel, of course," she retorted, in the vain hope that saying so would be enough
to validate such an outlandish claim. Even in her beleaguered frame of mind, though, she knew such an easy
escape was impossible until her grandmother was settled
again at Belvoir.

"Are you indeed?" he drawled. "And where exactly
are you planning to go?"

She sighed. Anywhere, as long as it's away from you,
she almost said, except that it wasn't true. She wanted
to be close to him, to breathe the same air, share the
same dreams. But she couldn't admit any of that, and
she'd taken the lie too far to back down now. "Back to
Boston."

"I see. May I ask why?"

"I have business to attend to." She flung the answer
at him, too overwrought to care that she was coming
across as cold and unfeeling. "I had a life back there,
in case you didn't realize, and it didn't simply grind to
a halt just because my grandmother needed me here."

That she could even entertain such callous thoughts,
let alone give voice to them, cut her to the quick. Why
was she reacting like this, as if she'd been coerced against
her will into returning to Belvoir? No one had pressured
her; it had been her decision. If she now felt trapped in
a situation she couldn't control, she had no one to blame
but herself.

Hadn't she known that, by coming back to the scene of her adolescent heartache, she was tempting fate to deal unkindly with her again? Of course she had!

Unfortunately, she'd also thought herself—her heart—safe. Only now, when it was too late to reverse the damage, did she realize she'd been wrong.

She was as helplessly in love with Lucas Flynn now, in all his moody, widowed misery, as she had been then when he was young and carefree. He might have discovered that the world was not his oyster after all, but he was still the pearl in hers.

The realization made her feel literally sick and she knew an urgent need to get away from him, out of the kitchen and into the sweet, fresh air of the garden.

But he stood in the doorway with his legs planted apart and his hands braced against the doorframe, and she knew that, even if she tried, she could not push past him and escape.

His eyes bored into hers, his mouth tight with determination and...could it be dismay?

"Forget it," he said, with very great certainty. "You're not going anywhere, Emily Jane. You're staying right here."

CHAPTER SIX

How easily the fantasy revived itself, springing alive more vibrantly than ever! "I'm not?" she said, her heart galloping in tremulous anticipation. "Why not, Lucas?"

"Because you're not leaving me to cope with your grandmother," he said crushingly. "Contrary to what you and she choose to believe, her health hangs by a very frail thread and I won't be held responsible for her total collapse when she learns of your defection."

How typical that he'd assume she would abandon Monique! "My grandmother," Emily declared, less because she wanted to argue the point than because she needed to buy enough time to conceal the disappointment wreaking havoc within her, "is a lot tougher than she looks. What makes you think my leaving for a few days will cause her to collapse?"

"What's suddenly come up in Boston that makes it so urgent for you to return there on the next available flight?"

"I have a job waiting."

"Really?" He raised a disbelieving brow. "Tell your boss you need compassionate leave."

"I *am* the boss," Emily said. "And my business won't run itself."

"Appoint a deputy," he replied, setting his mouth in an obstinate line.

She sighed, at a loss to understand why he should oppose her leaving when his whole attitude suggested he couldn't wait to see the back of her. "This isn't the script of some cheap Western, Lucas. I don't assign deputies and I don't expect my staff to handle my share of responsibility. They have enough to do dealing with their own, and this is a very busy time of year for us.''

"Really?" He gazed at her through narrowed eyes. "Exactly what sort of business are you running, Emily Jane, that your employees are too stressed out to pick up the slack when you're called away on a family emergency?"

"I own a planning agency," she said, choosing her words with care because she knew the scorn with which he'd react if she handed him her business card, which was how she usually introduced Done To Perfection. "We organize events."

"You mean like charity drives? Food banks and all that sort of stuff?" He looked marginally impressed for a change.

She sighed again and braced herself for the inevitable. "No. I mean I coordinate social events for people who are either unable or unwilling to do it for themselves. Weddings, anniversaries, dinner parties—that sort of thing."

"I see. And such events, of course, take precedence over your grandmother's precarious state of health, which is understandably not quite as critical a concern as orchestrating the canapés for some stranger's cocktail party." He favored her with the same scathing glance that he'd turned on her last night when she'd come back from her walk with Bruce. "It figures. You're as shallow and empty-headed now as you were at nineteen. I guess some things never change."

"How dare you sneer at me?" she flared, anger raging up to extinguish all the fond feelings for him that had resurrected themselves. "Where do you get off belittling what I do for a living when you don't have the first idea what it involves?"

"Educate me," he drawled. "Tell me how you lie awake nights worrying if the caviar is going to be up to scratch and the champagne properly chilled. Go ahead, Emily Jane. I'm all ears.''

"Those things are important, Lucas, just as much as your making sure you've got a tongue depressor handy when you need to examine a sore throat is important. But I don't denigrate the value of your work by focusing on minor details, and I'll thank you to afford me the same courtesy. For your information, I'm able to turn out a gourmet meal at the drop of a hat.''

"So is Beatrice.''

"You're right. But she didn't learn a sophisticated computer program so that she could keep track of her accounts, contracts, suppliers and inventory. She's never had more than two people working for her, whereas I have twenty full-time employees and a backup staff of twenty more for functions running to more than three hundred guests. I have learned the hospitality industry inside out, and am fully conversant with different cultural etiquettes. And if that isn't enough to convince you that I've graduated from teenage airhead into capable adult let me add that at least I make people happy, which is a damn sight more than can be said for you.''

He subjected her to a cool, sceptical stare. "And how did you reach that conclusion, Emily Jane? Is clairvoyance also a required talent in your line of work?''

"I don't need to be blessed with second sight to see that you're emotionally bankrupt, Lucas Flynn. There was a time when you'd have died rather than turn away from the people who needed you, yet look at you now, choosing to closet yourself in some sterile lab with a bunch of bacteria swimming around under a microscope because they won't make any demands on you!''

"That is not true." His words blazed across the kitchen, full of the kind of passion she wished he'd direct at her, and she noticed, belatedly, that he'd grown quite pale beneath his tan. "If anything, I care too damn much. Enough to devote my professional skills to re-

searching diseases which continue to take lives. Enough to weather the endless frustrations that go hand in hand with such work and to keep going despite the setbacks.''

"You don't care!" she cried, the hopeless, helpless longing clutching at her, tearing into her. "The only way you can relate to something with any sort of warmth or compassion is if it's growing in a petri dish!"

Astonishingly, after a moment's stunned silence he burst out laughing, and she could have kicked him. "Very good, Emily Jane! I'll have to remember that one the next time someone accuses me of letting my emotions interfere with my work!"

"Don't you laugh at me," she spat.

"And don't you go shooting your mouth off without knowing the facts," he said, sobering.

"The way you did when you told me so succinctly how trivial my career is, you mean?"

He shrugged. "OK, I asked for that. I'm sorry if I belittled your company. But that doesn't make it right for you to skip out on your grandmother at a time when she's feeling particularly vulnerable. For crying out loud, Emily Jane, you only just got here."

"I realize that, but I want—"

"We can't always have what we want," he cut in impatiently. "Sometimes, the price is just too high."

"I know," she shot back, exasperated that he wouldn't even give her the chance to justify her decision. "I wanted you once and paid dearly."

"And so did I. Or did you think I conveniently forgot that I'd had sex with one woman when I was engaged to another? I'm sorry that you were so hurt and guilt-ridden to find that you'd become pregnant, and regret more deeply than you'll ever know that you lost our child. If I'd realized at the time, I might have behaved differently. But I didn't, because you chose not to tell me. Instead, since I thought I couldn't give *you* what you wanted, I stuck to the commitment I could honor.

None of which has anything to do with your decision to abandon your grandmother when she is under great emotional and physical stress."

He spoke to her as if she were an undeserving sinner begging for penance. As if, despite his assertion to the contrary, she were completely without intelligence or moral conscience.

"I'm not going to abandon her!" Emily cried. "Nor did I mean to intimate I was, until you started spouting off about my fatal character flaws. Somehow, Lucas, you always manage to bring out the perverse in me."

"Then what are you planning to do about her?"

"Take her with me, I suppose," she said, wondering why she hadn't hit on such a logical solution sooner. "I've already decided my place is here with her, but I can't just leave my business affairs hanging in Boston. I have to go back and tie up the loose ends, and I don't see why it has to be such a problem. As long as my grandmother realizes we'll be away for only a short time, she might even enjoy herself and treat it like a holiday."

"You know she'll do no such thing."

"I know that I have to leave here."

"Because your job is so all-fired important," he said, with such withering contempt that she had to spit out the truth.

"No! Because I can't live under the same roof as you. I can't even live in the same town. It's just too painful."

"Painful how?"

"Too many reminders, Lucas. Too many old, unfulfilled hopes coming back to haunt me. I try to look on you as just another man but the fact remains that you're not. You're the man I fell in love with and who fathered my child. Running into you all the time is tearing me apart."

Just briefly, she thought he was going to agree with her, but at the last minute he swung away and rapped out a tattoo on the big pine table in the middle of the kitchen. "Your grandmother knows our history, doesn't she?"

"Some of it. She knows we were sexually involved, but she doesn't know I got pregnant. Nor does she know that I was the one who initiated . . . things."

"That explains her hostility." He turned back to face her again. "Surely you can see that, even if I offered to keep an eye on her while you're gone, she'd never accept me as her doctor? I'm the cad who deflowered her favorite grandchild. She'd rather be dead than take orders from someone like that. And make no mistake about it, Emily Jane, she will end up dead sooner rather than later unless she's properly supervised. Don't be taken in by how well she seems to cope. The only thing keeping her going is pride—and her determination to outlive Beatrice."

Before Emily could respond, a shadow fell across the threshold. "Oh, dear, I'm interrupting again." Tamara's tone managed a fine balance between regret and amusement.

Lucas heard only the regret. "Not at all," he said, bathing her in a smile that left Emily aching. "What can we do for you?"

Unable to look away, Emily watched with sick fascination as Tamara slid her hand under his elbow and nudged her breast against his arm. "There's something I wanted to discuss with you before I leave."

"You're leaving already?" Lucas inquired with palpable regret. "Why? What's your hurry?"

"I like to be home when my son gets out of school."

"I didn't know you were married," Emily said, snatching at the first piece of good news she'd had all day.

"I'm not." Tamara made a little moue of regret, pouting her full mouth into a perfect bee sting. "I'm that modern phenomenon, the single parent, trying to hold down a job and at the same time be a good mother."

"Very noble of you, I'm sure," Emily said waspishly. "What happened to the father?"

"Emily Jane!" Lucas made no effort to hide his annoyance. "Where the hell did *that* come from?"

"It's a reasonable enough question," she replied defiantly.

"It was unforgivably rude and none of your business."

"That's all right." Tamara hooked onto him more securely and turned a brave, saintly smile on Emily. "I'm a widow, sad to say."

"Oh." Confounded, Emily turned what was doubtless an unbecoming shade of red and mumbled, "I'm sorry."

"Thank you." Tamara inclined her head in gracious dismissal and focused her attention again on Lucas. "Now, I was wondering how you'd feel about...."

Her voice faded as she steered him through the door and back to the bright afternoon outside. Feeling thoroughly stymied at every turn, and more miserable than she'd thought it possible to be, Emily watched them go then slunk upstairs to her room.

She knew hiding away didn't resolve anything, that to sulk in solitude when things didn't go her way was juvenile to say the least. But the fact was, the past had come back to haunt her with such a vengeance that she again felt like the unhappy, bewildered teenager she'd once been.

Below her window, the murmur of voices rose and fell, interspersed with laughter and the clink of ice against crystal. Tamara, it seemed, had quite forgotten she had to be home in time for her son getting out of school.

Emily wasn't accustomed to being eaten alive by jealousy. In fact, the last time it had attacked had been the day Lucas had shown up at Belvoir with Sydney beside him, his ring flashing on the third finger of her left hand. But the passage of eleven years hadn't diminished its bite one bit, and Emily winced as it took hold again.

How was it that he always had patience to spare for others but never an ounce for her? All she had ever done was love him.

And did still. Despite everything.

The truth hit with the force of a blow from a blunt instrument. Muffling a groan, Emily buried her face in the pillow, dismayed beyond measure at the realization that, age and experience notwithstanding, she was as hopelessly addicted to Lucas Flynn as ever, no matter how hard he tried to break her of the habit.

He tried not to notice her absence at dinner. She was pouting and didn't deserve attention, he assured himself. She was also opinionated and ill-informed, not to mention rude. She'd do well to take a few lessons from Tamara in the art of social intercourse. And his giving a damn made no more sense than the irrational panic he'd felt earlier when she'd threatened to go back to Boston. If he had any sense of survival at all, he'd hasten her on her way. The less he saw of her the better.

That being the case, why did he find his gaze drawn repeatedly to her empty chair? Why did his heart threaten to cave in on itself when the picture of her almost taking a dive under the wheels of that red car yesterday replayed itself in his mind's eye? Why, for Pete's sake, did he have such an unholy urge to strip her naked and kiss the olive perfection of her skin?

Olive perfection of her skin?

He snorted quietly into his glass of wine and decided there was nothing more pitiful than a scientist trying to turn poet. Nor anything more embarrassing than the body's ability to respond contrary to the wishes of a person's mind. As his did, practically every time he allowed himself to think of her. It was ludicrous that a man his age should find himself at the mercy of erections the like of which he hadn't experienced since he was a callow youth of twenty.

"Does anyone know why Emily Jane hasn't come down for dinner?" he asked the table at large.

Old lady Lamartine fixed him with her malicious black gaze. "Quite possibly because certain people put her off her food."

"I peeped into her room and she was asleep," Bea said. "She looked worn out, poor thing, so I thought it best not to wake her, especially since she complained yesterday of a headache. I wonder, Lucas, if she might not be coming down with something."

He surprised himself then. "Unlikely," he said, "but if it'll ease your mind any I'll stop in and take a look at her to make sure."

"She won't appreciate that," her grandmother rapped out.

"I'll try to be too charming to resist," he said with unmasked irony. "Fix up a tray, Bea, and I'll use the excuse of bringing her a light supper to check up on her."

No sooner had he uttered the suggestion than he regretted it, in part because the light of curiosity in both grandmothers' eyes—Bea's inspired by hope, old lady Lamartine's by spite—was not something he intended to gratify. So he waited until the old ladies had retired for the night before embarking on a task which hindsight dictated was sheer folly.

He found Emily just as his grandmother had described. She'd flung her skirt and blouse over the foot of the bed but she hadn't bothered to climb under the sheets and lay covered only by the hand-crocheted bedspread.

A lamp burning on the chest of drawers near the fireplace touched her features with subdued color. In sleep her face was unbearably young and trusting, despite the dried tear tracks curving down her cheek.

She looked very slight under the cover, very fragile, and he knew again that clutch of terror at the realization of how easily her life could have been snuffed out yesterday. A second later, an inch or two closer, and the car....

Setting the tray on the nightstand, he eased himself down on the edge of the bed and rubbed a hand wearily over his face. What was wrong with him that he kept harping on the fact that she could have been hurt, instead of rejoicing in the fact that she'd escaped injury? As a doctor, he knew full well that focusing on the negative possibilities paved the way to the sort of major stress that cost a man his nerve when he most needed it. Just because he'd lost Sydney, that didn't mean he was going to lose—

The impact of where his thoughts were leading him brought him up short. Sydney had been his wife. How could he possibly see Emily Jane in that role? He didn't love her.

Did he?

Of course not! For Pete's sake, half the time he wasn't even sure he liked her. She was a pain in the butt—except when, absurdly, she caused him discomfort elsewhere.

His problem was, he'd been living like a monk for too long and he was not, by nature, the monastic type. Admittedly, sex hadn't played a very big part in his marriage—something he'd found difficult to accept at first, but he and Sydney had been close in other ways. A team, working side by side, year in and year out, medical missionaries so bloody dedicated to their work that they'd had little energy to spare for anything of a more intimate nature.

Well, now he had more time and freedom to do as he pleased, and if it pleased him to satisfy his sexual appetites there were plenty of women who'd be happy to accommodate him—starting with Tamara Golding, who'd made it plain she was available whenever he felt the urge. He certainly, *definitely* was not about to deceive himself into thinking Emily Jane Lamartine was the solution to what ailed him, and never mind how hard his body tried to tell him differently!

The shift in her breathing and the slight movement in the mattress alerted him to her awakening. Looking down, he saw that her eyes were open and fixed unblinkingly on him.

"You were crying," he said.

"Was I?" Her voice floated up to him, gravelly with sleep.

"Yes." Involuntarily, his finger traced a path up the baby-fine skin of her cheek. "Is it your headache?"

The look she turned on him, so full of honesty and reproach, filled him with shame. "No," she said. "It's you."

She had always been like that—spilling out the truth regardless of the consequences. Saying things better left unsaid and never once apologizing for doing so. If he were to allow himself the same luxury, he'd admit that that was one of the qualities he'd always found irresistible in her.

Instead, he called on the thing he did best: turning away from what he preferred not to face. "How so?"

"I want so badly to please you," she said, trapping his hand beneath hers when he went to remove it from her cheek. "To make you happy, to bring you back to life."

"I'm not exactly dead, Emily," he said raggedly, once again reminded that even her most innocuous touch was enough to beleaguer him with embarrassment. "And it isn't your job to make me happy."

She let go of him to push herself up on one elbow. "Even if that's what I want, more than anything else in the world?" she pleaded, leaning toward him.

She was wearing only a slip, one strap of which had fallen off her shoulder. Not all the self-control in the world could stop his eyes from tracking a path past the swatch of cream lace skimming her breasts to the suggestion of cleavage beneath, and even he, master of self-deceit that he'd become, knew he was teetering on the brink of a desire that would not be satisfied with a mere glimpse.

He wanted to touch, to taste. God help him, he wanted *her* and could no longer deny it.

Swallowing, he tore his gaze away. "Don't do this, Emily," he said hoarsely. "Don't push me into something we'll both hate me for tomorrow."

In one graceful movement she rose to kneel before him and framed his face in her hands, forcing him to look at her. At her huge, beautiful brown eyes, at her ripe, sweet mouth. "I could never hate you, Lucas," she murmured, weaving her fingers into his hair.

"No?" He summoned up the travesty of a laugh and tried to will his defiant flesh into submission. He might as well have tried to tame a raging bull. "You could have fooled me. You don't seem terribly impressed by the man I've become."

"It's the man you are underneath that matters. He's the one I've always loved."

He watched her mouth, hypnotized as much by its shape and movement as by its words. She had always been feminine, even as a little girl. Now she was womanly, too. Overflowing with sensual warmth. Soft, alluring.

He ached to sink himself into that warmth, to feel her softness close around him and hold him prisoner.

"That man doesn't exist any more, Emily," he replied unevenly. "He lost part of his soul in a hell-hole of a world you can't begin to comprehend."

"Did he?" she whispered, further narrowing the space that separated her from him. Her pupils gleamed in the twilight, huge dark mirrors that reflected the turbulence of his emotions amid the calm certainty of hers. "Are you sure?"

What did he know about sure? He'd thought he was sure about medicine, about devoting himself to the care of others, about making a life with Sydney in that god-forsaken country in Africa. And in the end he'd gone sour on all of them and buried his ideals along with his wife. He'd have to be crazy to let Emily convince him otherwise.

"I'm sure," he said, turning away from a possibility too outlandish to merit consideration, no matter how hard it hammered to be heard.

"So am I," she said, and closed the last gap between them.

Her mouth came up to his and captured it with sweet conviction. Her lips were warm and mobile, seducing him despite his best efforts to resist her.

The other strap of her slip was a thread of satin against the pure silk of her shoulder. Under his guidance, it whispered down her arm, leaving her naked from the waist up except for a flimsy little bra.

Of course, he shouldn't have touched her, hadn't intended to. But the second her mouth fused with his he found himself so avid for a repeat of the pleasure she'd brought him once before, a long time ago, that nothing else counted. Passion blazed, pushing him to the brink of control.

Even then, he might have withstood the temptation of her. But, in a gesture that was at once audacious and artlessly generous, she took his hands and brought his palms to press against her breasts. He felt her heart fluttering erratically and saw the craving that tortured him cloud her eyes also.

He saw the way her head fell back to leave her throat exposed and vulnerable to whatever he chose to inflict on it. The upsurge of emotion that simple gesture created stirred him to a different kind of turmoil, one which suggested that perhaps he hadn't lost his soul, after all.

"Emily...!" He sighed her name in an agony of wanting that left his throat raw.

With that one word, he surrendered, admitting to himself and to her that she'd been right all along: he'd never dealt honestly with his feelings where she was concerned. He could no more resist her than he could stop breathing.

But she heard denial in the way he breathed her name. "Don't," she begged in a fractured whisper. "Don't spoil it by talking. You don't have to say anything, Lucas— no promises you can't keep, no words you don't mean." Her hands fluttered over him, identifying the hunger and need he couldn't disguise. "Just let us have tonight. Let me give myself to you, please. Just this once, don't deny us what we both want so badly."

"At least I make people happy..which is more than can be said of you!"

Her words from that afternoon sliced through the haze befuddling his mind, clearing a path for the self-righteous voice of conscience to speak its piece.

Hadn't he known, when he'd offered to visit her room, that, ultimately, this was what he'd come for? To ease the ache she provoked, knowing she would never refuse him? Hadn't his entire being hummed with covert anticipation over the course of the long, slow evening until, by the time he pushed her door closed behind him, he'd been no better than a dog sniffing out a bitch in heat?

Yes, yes, and yes! The truth was too painfully plain even for him to ignore. He was nothing but a louse to take advantage of her like this.

She sensed his retreat immediately and tried to halt it, winding her arms around his neck and seeking his mouth once more, as if she thought that if she could kiss him deeply enough he'd forget his reservations.

She very nearly succeeded. Her lips softened, parted, and it took more self-control than he could command to reject what she offered. He tasted her mouth, learned its sweet, dark secrets, let his tongue show in graphic imitation how he would like to possess the rest of her.

Deep in her throat she answered him with a soft little purr of acquiescence, and disgust at his own self-indulgence flooded through him again, stripping him of passion. "No!" he groaned, tearing himself away.

Her eyes, which moments earlier had been misty with passion, turned dark with misery. "Oh, Lucas, why not?"

He shook his head, at a loss to convey to her a discovery he was having a tough time accepting himself. He had thought he was immune to her and only tonight had realized how badly he needed her and how little he deserved her.

Misreading the situation entirely, she let out a soft sigh of defeat and said plaintively, "You don't want me."

He couldn't bear her distress. The poignancy in her eyes, her voice ripped him apart. "I want you," he admitted roughly, "but damn it, I can't use you. Another woman perhaps, one who isn't ready to give me her all and ask nothing in return, but not you, Emily. Not after everything else I've put you through."

"I'm still not woman enough, is that it?"

"That's not it at all!" He ran a frustrated hand through his hair and wished he hadn't tried explaining to her something still so new and unsettling to himself that it left his brain addled. "You're different, special. But the hell of it is I'm only just beginning to concede you always have been, from the very first. Call me pig-headed—or, if it makes you feel better, a bloody coward—for not having the guts to acknowledge the fact sooner."

The light came on again in her eyes. "Then doesn't that make everything simpler, Lucas?"

Rationally, it should have. He ought to have been able to please them both without a qualm. Except that doing so would leave her more bereft than ever because, until he was certain he could give her the sort of commitment he knew she both wanted and needed, what had he to offer her, once tonight was over?

"Look at me," he said, taking her hands firmly in his. "This afternoon you accused me of lacking warmth and compassion for people, of being emotionally bankrupt. I'm still that same man, Emily. Nothing's changed since then."

Her shoulders sagged. "So what are you saying? That we have no future together?"

He looked away because he couldn't bear to watch her eyes grow opaque with pain again. "I'm not sure you can be happy with me. Until I am, I'm not prepared to let things go any further between us."

"What if I don't ask for more than you can already give?"

"But you will," he said tenderly, drawing his fingertip over her trembling mouth. "You won't be able to help it because, unlike me, you've never turned away from the truth about yourself. And the fact is, your priorities aren't mine. *Things* don't matter to me the way they do to you. I don't care about money or prestige. It doesn't bother me to drive a ten-year-old car as long as it gets me where I want to go."

A spark of anger flared in her eyes. "Do you think I'm so shallow and materialistic that I judge a man's worth by the make and model of the car he drives?"

"No," he said. "But nor do I think you should have to change your standards to accommodate mine. The fact is, I've moved on. In a way I *am* as emotionally detached as you accused me of being. I have to be to deal with the global misery caused by disease, otherwise I'd go mad with the grief of it all. My work matters to me, Emily. At times it consumes me to the exclusion of everything else. It's always been enough for me, but I'm not such a fool as to believe it would be enough for you."

"It would," she whispered. "As long as you were mine some of the time, it would be enough."

"Not over the long haul," he said, and drew a long, ragged breath. "You'd want more, and if I can't give it where does that leave us? A person can compromise only so far. Believe me, I know. I made a lot of concessions during my marriage and lived to resent many of them."

"But you loved Sydney!"

"Not enough," he said, wincing as the truth he'd steadfastly refused to recognize erupted within him like an abscess that had festered for years. "I don't think I could live with myself if I were to do the same to you, Emily."

The tears rolled down her face in a silent flood. "I don't know what to do to make you change your mind," she wailed, sitting there with her designer slip crumpled around her and looking for all the world like the little girl he used to know.

But she wasn't a girl any more, she was a woman who knew what she wanted and had the courage to go after it. And he was damned if he'd shortchange her. Until he was sure he could give her everything she needed from a relationship, he could offer her only tonight. And she deserved a lot more than that.

"I cannot give you what you want, not right now," he said.

"What if I can't wait any longer?" she wept.

"Then you'll let go of the past and move forward without me, and the loss will be mine."

"How can you be so calm? Doesn't it scare you, just a little bit, to risk losing me like that?"

"Oh, darling Emily," he murmured, folding her in his arms, "it scares me more than you can begin to imagine."

"You can't possibly be more afraid than I am," she sobbed, soaking his shirtfront.

He pushed her hair away from her face and fought the quiver of desire that persisted in tugging at his groin. "Yes, I can," he said. "Because you know who you are but I've become a stranger, not just to everyone who ever cared about me but to myself as well. I have to find myself again, Emily. Find the man under the white coat and see if he can function as a whole person outside his lab."

"Do you think that's possible?" Her eyes implored him.

How much simpler it would be just to make the promise they both wanted to hear and hope to high heaven he could live up to it! To tell her that everything would work out and they could build together the future that she yearned for.

"If it is, I'll come to you and hope you see the man you've always thought I was."

"I don't need to wait to find that out. I'll take my chances now."

He kissed the top of her head, then stepped away from the bed before his resolve melted. "No, you won't," he said. "You deserve better than having to settle for second best. If we have any chance of a future together, it has to be one in which we both invest equally. And I promise you that if there's a way for us to do that I'll find it."

CHAPTER SEVEN

IF EMILY had thought that that night would change everything between her and Lucas for the better, the next morning showed her it wasn't going to happen quite that quickly or easily. He behaved much as he usually did on those days when he worked out of the house, going out to the patio and immersing himself in the morning paper the moment breakfast was over.

Beatrice pottered about, watering her flower tubs and pinching back the blooms on the heliotrope, while Monique positioned her wheelchair in such a way that Emily had to lean forward to sneak a look at Lucas—a move which didn't escape her grandmother's inquisitive gaze. And then Tamara Golding showed up, swanning around the corner of the house as if she owned the place.

After a blithe, "Good morning, ladies," she perched herself on the arm of Lucas's chair, and if she didn't go quite so far as to drape herself all over him it was so clearly what she'd have liked to do that she might as well have worn a placard around her neck stating the fact. As for Lucas...!

Emily swallowed the knot of outrage clogging her throat. No one would have guessed he'd come close to saying he loved her just a few hours ago. In fact, if the way he eventually cloistered himself at the far end of the patio with the widow Golding was any indication, he'd probably undergone an overnight change of heart.

The only sign that anything had altered between him and Emily was that his manner had lost something of its reserved edge. When she made so bold as to interrupt his low, intense conversation with Tamara to offer the guest coffee, he actually smiled. As if he liked her. After last night, though, liking wasn't enough for Emily.

It was, however, entirely too much for Monique, who witnessed the exchange with unvarnished displeasure. "It would be nice," she pronounced irritably, "if people around here could direct their sympathies toward the less fortunate occasionally. Apparently no one has noticed that my precious Robespierre has not been in evidence since the night of the mishap at Belvoir, and while that might not disturb the serenity of your days it is certainly impairing mine."

Unable to drag her attention away from the shining blond head bent so attentively close to Lucas's thick, dark mop of hair, Emily said absently, "I'm sure Robespierre is just fine, Grand-mère. Cats are very independent creatures."

"But *I* am not fine," Monique snapped. "I am distressed, and that is not good for a woman in my condition. Since I am confined to a wheelchair and therefore unable to go searching for him myself, I would appreciate it, Emily Jane, if you would bestir yourself to find him and bring him here to me so that he knows he has not been abandoned."

"Can't it wait?" Emily said, reluctant to leave Tamara such a clear field.

"No, it cannot," Monique declared, flinging Lucas a poisonous glare.

He didn't notice. He was too engrossed in his furtive little conference with Tamara, which had progressed to the stage where she had her hand resting urgently on his wrist. Emily could have strangled the pair of them.

She sighed. "All right, Grand-mère, if it'll make you feel better."

"It will." Monique's tone left the matter in no doubt.

Unable to resist one last shot at ridding herself of such a determined rival, Emily said, with rather more belligerence than grace, "Goodbye, Tamara. You'll probably be gone before I get back."

"Perhaps." Tamara tossed out the reply, barely missing a beat in her conversation.

Lucas flicked a faintly surprised glance in Emily's direction but didn't see fit to comment.

Just as well, she thought a few minutes later, marching savagely across Roscommon's back lawn and armed with a pillowcase to contain the cat in the event that she found him. One word of reproach from her almost-lover and she'd have lost it completely!

The sun glinted dully off the smoke-blackened windows of Belvoir's main salon but the sounds of activity echoing from within indicated that repair and restoration were already under way.

Robespierre was not a sociable cat so it was unlikely he'd be anywhere near the house, but he was a creature of habit and very fond of his comforts. Cutting across the neglected rose garden, Emily made her way toward the wall of shrubbery that separated Monique's home from the Barretts', her neighbors on the other side. Bathed in morning sunlight, it was reputedly one of Robespierre's favorite basking spots.

Call and coax though she might, however, the cat did not appear, nor was he prowling in the long, sweet grass growing along the water's edge. That left only the belvedere, which was situated beyond sight and sound of the main house and commanded a view of the river as it flowed downstream and rounded the curve past Roscommon.

From all appearances, the structure had stood abandoned since the summer Emily had watched and waited so hopelessly for Lucas to come and declare himself. The ornate wrought iron of its domed roof and trellises was powdered with rust, its floor littered with leaves and the assorted debris of many winters.

Once, the curved benches inside had been covered with striped canvas, but the fabric had long since rotted. All that was left were the crumbling remains of the cushions, which, judging from the tufts of kapok sticking out at intervals, had been home to a family of rodents for quite some time.

Not the sort of place a person might want to linger, it was nonetheless definitely one which presented good hunting opportunities for a hungry cat. Wrinkling her nose at the musty odor which not even the sweet air of a northern Californian spring could eliminate, Emily picked her way up the shallow flight of steps to the shaded interior of the summerhouse.

It wasn't just the smell of disuse that permeated the atmosphere, it was the aura of dejection accompanying it that resurrected another wave of memories so pain-filled that Emily's throat ached. Tomb-like in its privacy, this was a sad place, a place where things had died.

She had come here to count off the days and ultimately face, with sick dread, the fact that she was nineteen, pregnant and single, with no wedding plans looming on the horizon to mitigate the situation because the love of her life was marrying another woman.

Somewhere among the withered leaves crumbling under her feet lay the forgotten bits and pieces of her heart which she had never quite managed to put back together again after Lucas had broken it so thoroughly.

She'd wanted to die that long-ago summer, but had been too cowardly to do anything to expedite the matter. She supposed she ought to be glad of that now, with things between her and him seeming so much brighter.

Except what had he really promised her?

She leaned against a trellis and stared moodily at the peaceful garden. He'd promised her nothing but a lot of maybes that might never amount to anything. *Would* never amount to anything if Tamara Golding had her way, and Emily was far too finely attuned to the other woman's agenda not to recognize that she was the type who wouldn't easily be put to rout.

"Think about it," she muttered glumly, coughing a little at the cloud of dust that rose up when she plopped herself down on the rotting cushions of the nearest bench. "She's pulling out all the stops, parading her widowhood and worthiness for all the world to see. A sex-starved divorcée whose career aspirations revolve around other people's soirées and parties hardly paints an admirable picture by comparison—and you might as well face it, Emily Lamartine, that pretty well sums up how Lucas perceived you until you set him straight."

A rustling at the end of the bench startled her into silence. Seconds later, some sort of field mouse poked its head out from behind the cushion. A pretty little thing with big round ears, it stopped halfway out of its nest, its nose twitching as it sniffed out the danger spelled by an intruder.

Whatever other neuroses she had, Emily had never been one to squeal with fright over insects or rodents. To have done so, with the six Flynn boys living next door every summer, would have spelled endless misery. "Don't run away on my account," she said now as the mouse pinned her with a terrified, beady little gaze. "I'm as much an outcast around here as you."

But when even the mouse didn't relish her company and flitted back into its hole she decided she'd wasted enough time feeling sorry for herself and would be better occupied trying to shape a future more tolerable than the unhappy past. "A future which doesn't include Tamara Golding's cool, amused voice and sleek golden limbs," she declared to the scarlet bougainvillaea climbing up the trellis, and just about screamed with shock when a voice from behind answered.

"Talking to yourself, Emily?" Bruce's pleasant baritone was laced with amusement. "Doesn't say much for the company at Roscommon, does it?"

Unsure how much he'd overheard, Emily chose to brazen it out. "Actually, I was talking to a mouse," she said, standing up and brushing flecks of kapok from her skirt. "Come in and wait for him to pop out of his nest again. He's the cutest little thing, with ears like parachutes."

Eyeing the derelict belvedere, Bruce stationed himself against one of the entrance posts and gave a comical shudder. "No, thanks! I wouldn't have thought this was your idea of a pleasant place to spend the morning, either."

"I came looking for Robespierre."

"I think he died a couple of hundred years ago." Bruce's amusement erupted into laughter that was too infectious to resist.

"Not this one," she said, joining in. "He's my grandmother's fourteen-year-old cat and he hasn't been seen since the fire." Then she stopped and looked at Bruce curiously. "But how did you know where to find me?"

"I saw you from the Barretts' garden. Is this cat you're looking for a big male tabby with an unpleasant addiction to clawing the ankles of passing strangers?"

"You've found him!"

"He's taken up residence under the Barretts' front verandah."

"Oh, my grandmother *will* be pleased! Can I count on you to help me catch him?"

Bruce bathed her in another endearing grin. "I'd rather tackle California's most wanted criminal! But if you'll do the trapping I'll show you exactly where he's holed up."

Robespierre took some persuading but eventually, and with the added lure of a can of sardines provided by Bruce's hostess, they finally captured him. Although her grandmother was delighted to have him back again, when she showed up with him on the patio and found Tamara still holding court, Emily realized she didn't know the half of it when it came to trapping.

As if cornering one man wasn't enough, the moment she set eyes on Bruce Tamara corralled him, as well. "Oh, wonderful; you've saved me having to come looking for you!" she exclaimed, then, with one of her charming little grimaces, added, "Come and join the discussion that's raging by all means, but promise me you won't take as long to convince as Lucas."

"Can anyone join in?" Emily asked tartly, and was promptly rewarded for her nastiness.

"Not really, dear," Tamara cooed. "This isn't something that exactly concerns you—at least not right now."

And how exactly does it concern you? Emily wondered, quelling the homicidal urge to choke Tamara for the patronising attitude she dished out.

Monique prevented any sort of retaliation, however, by announcing, "Emily Jane, I wish to have a few words with you in private. Be so good as to wheel me to my room."

Once there, she came straight to the point. "You're lusting after that Flynn creature again, aren't you, Emily Jane? It's as plain as the green in your eyes every time you look at Madame Golding."

"Yes," Emily said, too discouraged to bother denying what must be patently obvious to the most casual observer.

Monique stroked Robespierre, who purred contentedly on her lap, and pursed her lips before replying. When she finally spoke, her tone was surprisingly mild. "You know, *ma chère,* I had hoped you'd outgrown him. You assured me you had, if you recall, the day you arrived at Belvoir. But of far graver import is the way he now looks at you. As if, for the first time, he actually sees you. I find that very unsettling, Emily Jane. Frightening, in fact."

"It's how he looks at Tamara Golding that upsets me," Emily confessed.

"He is a man," Monique said bitterly. "When did you ever know one capable of withstanding the attentions of an attractive woman, especially one who flings herself at him so shamelessly? Give him the chance and he will break your heart over and over again. Perhaps your remaining here with me is not such a good idea, after all."

So Monique saw it too—that filament of attraction to Tamara that Lucas was either unable or unwilling to sever. Emily looked at her grandmother, at the concern and love she saw written on her face, and her eyes filled with tears.

Monique gave a sigh and reached for her hand. "So, it is already too late. I was afraid that might be the case."

"What shall I do, Grand-mère?" Emily whimpered pathetically.

"There is but one of two things you can do, *ma chère*. You can cut him out of your heart as you would a disease, or you can fight for him. Only you can decide which of the two will bring you the least pain. And I can do nothing but watch and wait, just as I did the last time, and hope he does not destroy you."

Emily had known all along what her course of action was going to be, of course. Her grandmother's assessment merely confirmed her decision. "I gave in without a fight before and it destroyed me anyway," she said. "This time, I'll follow my instincts and confront the situation head-on."

A grudging respect illuminated Monique's dark eyes. "You are a true Lamartine, Emily Jane. A woman after my own heart, to be sure. Although I defy anyone to persuade me the man deserves your love, in a strange kind of way I'm proud of your decision. It makes up for my own lack of courage a long time ago, when I faced a similar threat."

At the time, it did not occur to Emily to question the reasoning behind that remark. It was enough to know that at least one person in the house was on her side.

She didn't get a chance to speak to Lucas alone until early afternoon. Beatrice had asked Bruce and Tamara to stay for lunch—an invitation which they'd both accepted and which left Emily wondering if they'd be moving in with their toothbrushes before much longer. When Tamara tried to claim the chair closest to Lucas, however, Monique blocked her path, maneuvering her wheelchair with such fearsome skill that she almost ran the woman down. "Help me to the table, please," she ordered. "I am incapacitated, as I'm sure you can see."

Seizing the opportunity, Emily slid into the vacant seat and murmured, "What is it that's kept you so busy all morning, Lucas?"

He shrugged. "Oh, just some wild idea that Tamara's come up with. Nothing that would interest you, Emily."

She was in no mood to be put off with that sort of answer. If their relationship was to stand any sort of chance, it had to be based on equality and sharing. "Anything that concerns you interests me," she replied rashly, "especially when it involves such close and prolonged consultation with the widow Golding."

He had been about to take a sip of water, but, at her remark, he rested the heavy crystal glass on the table and subjected her to a penetrating gaze. "Are you trying to crowd me, Emily? To pressure me a little, because of what transpired between us last night?"

"Don't I have the right?" she shot back in a low voice. "Or was what transpired between us last night just a diversionary tactic on your part?"

His gorgeous blue eyes took on a flinty cast. "At this stage, neither of us has any *rights* concerning the other, Emily Jane. All that exists between us is possibilities, and they're hardly likely to flourish in a climate of jealousy and distrust."

Last night he'd called her Emily, and she'd taken it as a sign that at last he saw her as the woman she'd become and not still as the girl she'd once been. But here he was, harking back to Emily Jane again, and it was that revealing little slip of the tongue that undid her.

"Don't talk to me as if I were a child, Lucas Flynn," she whispered, almost blinded by a combination of rage and dismay.

"Then stop behaving like one," he replied cuttingly. "And for Pete's sake stop making a scene, because I won't stand for it."

"Is there a problem at your end of the table?" Tamara's dulcet tones floated down to them, riddled with malicious curiosity.

Of course, Lucas didn't pick up on that and took the question at face value. "Yes," he said bluntly, the fingers still wrapped tightly around his glass uncurling a little. "Emily Jane wants to know what we've been talking about all morning. Perhaps, for all our sakes, you'd better tell her. In fact, she might be just the person you need to help you out with that catering problem you mentioned."

Tamara gazed at him commiseratingly. "I don't suppose it can do any harm. Dear," she trilled, studiously addressing the wall behind Emily, "the April Valley Winery hosts a sort of community social event every year at which we honor certain people for their contributions to the well-being of our town. A sort of formal thank-you, if you like, for services above and beyond the call of duty. And I've spent the entire morning, plus a good portion of yesterday afternoon, trying to convince Lucas that he deserves recognition for the part he played in saving that lovely old house next door from burning to the ground."

She paused delicately. "And Bruce too, of course. As far as those of us on the selection committee are concerned, they're both local heroes."

She smiled the whole time but the undertone of her little spiel suggested the men would have deserved even greater reward if they'd seen fit to leave certain inhabitants of Belvoir to fry.

"Problem is, they've hit some sort of snag with the people who usually supply the dinner," Lucas put in. "Something to do with a labor dispute that's got half the staff on strike, didn't you say, Tamara?"

"I'm afraid so, and it's looking very much as if the problem isn't going to be resolved any time soon, so we're scrambling to find another caterer to take over—not an easy task with so little lead time."

"Well, Emily Jane, what do you say?" Lucas turned to her with an indescribably smug expression on his all too handsome face. "Here's your chance to strut your stuff."

"I'm hardly equipped to jump into the middle of something as big as a banquet, Lucas, with neither staff nor suppliers to call on."

"Well, darling, of course you are!" Beatrice cried. "With a bit of local help, you'll put that old catering company to shame! Tell us what's involved, Tamara."

"A five course gourmet meal, a sampling of fine local wines, a few speeches, a smattering of polite applause, and then the actual presentations." Tamara gave one of her deliberate little pauses, then added blandly, "Nothing that a person on her own would care to tackle, I'm afraid."

She might as well have come right out and said, Nothing that I'm interested in having you get involved in, Emily Lamartine, but Beatrice killed the insinuation before it could take root.

"Nonsense!" she scoffed. "She'll manage beautifully. A marvellous evening it is, Emily, darling. Started about five years ago as I recall, with everyone who's anyone in April Water there to lend support, and a grand opportunity for us all to dress to the nines.''

''I can't possibly take advantage of Emily Jane like that,'' Tamara said rather shortly. ''We'll have someone come up from the city. San Francisco's full of excellent gourmet suppliers.''

Although she knew she'd live to regret it when the realities had to be dealt with, Emily couldn't let well enough alone. Turning her sweetest smile on Tamara, she purred, ''Don't be silly. I wouldn't miss the opportunity to orchestrate the banquet, any more than I'd dream of missing the rest of the evening, especially since Lucas and Bruce are to be honored. How lovely of you to think of nominating them.''

Lucas sort of choked at that, while Tamara merely looked as if she might. It wasn't until after lunch, when the grandmothers were taking a siesta and Emily was busy loading the dishwasher, that Tamara caught up with her. ''You forgot this,'' she said, slamming through the swinging door into the kitchen and plunking the soup tureen down on the pine table.

''So I did,'' Emily said, knowing full well that Tamara's appearance had nothing at all to do with good housekeeping. ''Thanks for bringing it in.''

''My pleasure, dear. Kitchens always interest me. They say so much about the people who work in them, don't you think?''

She looked around at the polished copper pots hanging from the ceiling and the braids of garlic strung from an iron rack on the wall, then brought her gaze back to bear on Emily with the pity of one inspecting a singularly unfortunate Cinderella. ''Which brings me to something else which I think must be said. I know you came out here on a mission of mercy, as it were, to do something about your poor old grandma, so I can quite see that you wouldn't be prepared for anything quite as . . . elegant, shall we say, as this evening at the winery that we were talking about at lunch."

"Not any more than I was expecting Belvoir to go up in flames," Emily said.

"Exactly. And since I'm sure you wouldn't want to be embarrassed I think I ought to warn you that, parochial though we are in many ways, Mrs. Flynn was quite right when she said that people here treat the event seriously enough to dress . . . appropriately."

Her glance raked over Emily, taking in the same cotton skirt she'd worn the day before with mingled pity and distaste. "I mean no offence, dear, when I say that your wardrobe would seem rather unsuitable for the occasion. S-o-o . . ." She drew out the word on a gust of regret. "Although I'm sure we can supply you with a little black dress and white apron if you *insist* on working in the kitchen I really don't think, all other things considered, that you'd be comfortable in anything other than a . . . subservient role, do you?"

Too nonplussed by the woman's gall to do anything else, Emily simply stared at her.

"Of course, you could always go out and buy something that would do, if you're determined to insinuate yourself into the party."

"Of course," Emily murmured faintly.

"But it seems rather pointless, don't you think, considering you're an outsider with no real involvement in the community? And quite frankly I don't normally expect my hired help to mingle with the guests except in a—ah—*working* capacity."

The whole scene smacked so blatantly of a badly written soap opera that Emily almost laughed. "I don't consider myself an outsider, Tamara," she said. "My grandmother is a prominent member of April Water society and has been for years. As for being your hired help—"

"But this isn't to do with your grandmother, Emily, except very peripherally," Tamara interjected smoothly. "It's to do with the Flynns, who are not related to you."

"They have been part of my life for as long as I can remember. My connections with them—and, in fact, with the town in general—go back a very long way." She slid the last plate into the dishwasher, snicked closed the door, and said pointedly, "I don't recall ever hearing your name mentioned before this summer, though. When did you come to April Water, Tamara?"

"Three years ago, shortly after my husband died. I felt the need to leave unhappy memories behind and make a fresh start."

"I came back here for the same reason."

"I see. And I suppose," Tamara said, with more than a hint of venom, "that horning in on our annual event qualifies as part of your rehabilitation?"

"Absolutely. One of my problems in the past, you see, was giving up too easily on those things that really mattered to me. I intend to rectify that while I'm here."

"In that case, it would appear that we have nothing more to say to each other."

"Indeed not," Emily said. "Always assuming, of course, that we were talking about the same thing to begin with."

Tamara's eyes narrowed. "Oh, I think we both know that we were, Emily Jane, which is why I took the precaution of inviting Lucas to be my guest that evening. I'm so sorry, dear, that there won't be room for you at our table, except for those times when you're serving us, of course."

Oh, lady! Emily thought, grinding her molars in rage. Keep this up and I'll shove you in the oven, then serve you as the main course—Done To Perfection!

Lucas had planned to drive into the city and spend the afternoon in the lab, but he knew he'd never be able to concentrate on the correlation of his latest test results when he had so many other, personal concerns on his mind. So, he cleaned out Roscommon's old wooden eaves troughs instead, replacing sections that were rotted and climbing up and down ladders until his legs were about ready to drop off. At least the activity left his mind free to grapple with what was really bothering him.

The fact was that when Emily had blown back into his life he'd been jolted out of the snug little niche he'd carved for himself and forced to join the mainstream of life again. All those wounds he'd brought back from Africa had grown tired of festering and started healing of their own accord. Life held excitement again. The past, which he'd once thought would haunt him for ever, was fading rapidly and the future shone bright with sudden promise. Even his work had taken on fresh challenge, despite his playing hookey from it today.

Like a severely frostbitten man exposed to heat, the feeling had trickled back, a slow, painful transition that had begun at his extremities and gradually worked up to his heart. And he knew it had to do with her, with her zest for living and her infinite capacity to love and forgive. She was the antidote to everything his life had become over the last eleven years.

The question was, as he'd told her last night, could he offer her what she both needed and deserved? Was he really ready to clear this last hurdle and make the emotional commitment without which no serious relationship stood a ghost of a chance, or was a belated sense of guilt driving him?

He rammed a last section of new eaves troughing into place and stared at his handiwork. A bead of sealant, a coat of paint, and no one would ever see where the damage had been cut away. Sort of like Emily, who showed no visible scars at all for what he'd put her through. But that didn't change the fact that she'd lost his baby, or that perhaps it needn't have happened if he'd been there to take care of her. They might have been the parents of a ten-year-old son or daughter if he'd done the honorable thing and married her eleven years ago.

Marriage. The word sent chills down his spine. Not because of its finality, but because he knew, deep down, that he'd royally screwed up the first time around. And Emily hadn't fared much better. Were they crazy even to contemplate jumping in a second time? And if they were, where did they go from here?

For him, the safest place was probably up this ladder until he figured out the next step, because, in all truth, he was afraid to be alone with her. She was too alluring for him to resist, even when she was being unreasonable, as she had been at lunch.

He thought of little but making love to her. Awoke in a sweat most nights, the dream of her lying naked beneath him so vivid that it took every ounce of restraint he could muster not to race into her bedroom and give in to the agony.

"Lucas, do you intend to spend the rest of the day up that ladder, or will you come down and join us for the cocktail hour?" Bea's voice floated up, filled with frustration.

She'd been very unhappy with his decision to isolate himself all afternoon. She'd wanted to spend the time discussing ad nauseam the great honor the town was so anxious to heap on him. He hoped she'd got the idea out of her system by now, but, either way, he could hardly spend the whole night hanging from the roof and hoping the exercise would be enough to deaden his libido.

"I'm about done for the day," he called back. "Give me another ten minutes and I'll be down."

His hair was still damp from a shower and he'd nicked himself shaving when he came out to join the three women half an hour later. They were sitting under the walnut tree, deep in discussion. Old lady Lamartine had her cat on her lap, Bea had brought out her embroidery, and Emily reclined in a lawn chair with a notepad propped on her knees.

"It simply isn't a problem, darling," Bea was saying.

"What isn't?" he asked, dropping down on the grass beside Emily.

"Emily's worrying about finding reliable help for the banquet, but I'm sure the Ladies' League can give her some names," his grandmother replied, scotching any hope he'd had that the topic had worn itself out.

"I think my granddaughter should turn the job over to the Golding woman," old lady Lamartine declared. "Not that anyone bothered to ask my opinion, of course, but had they done so I'd have been more than happy to point out that Lamartines are not accustomed to being treated as servants."

"Drawing up a menu and orchestrating a meal isn't exactly hard labor, Grand-mère," Emily said lazily, stretching her arms above her head in such a way that the outline of her breasts beneath the pink blouse she wore was gilded with sunlight. "I enjoy it. I'd just feel more comfortable dealing with people who've worked with me before and who know how I like things to be done."

"You don't belong in the kitchen," her grandmother grumbled. "Your place is with me, seated well above the salt."

"And that's where I'll be, if it's at all possible. The thing is, I didn't come prepared for a formal function, and I'm not sure I'll find time to drive into San Francisco to shop for a dress."

Beatrice decided to put in another two cents' worth at that. "But there's no need, Emily Jane! The wardrobe in your room is full of lovely things from the days when I was as slim as you, and those fashions are all the rage again now."

"What a very novel idea," Monique Lamartine said snidely. "Wearing someone else's cast-offs to attend an important social function on the arm of a man of Bruce Anderson's stature! I confess such a thought never would have occurred to me."

"He asked you to go with him?" Lucas asked, too outraged to care that he sounded like a dog snarling over a bone.

"Is there a reason he shouldn't?" Emily asked innocently. "You agreed to go with Tamara, after all."

He should have seen that one coming and ducked! "You're right," he said. "And that reminds me that I'll have to haul out my old dinner jacket and hope it still fits, in which case we'll both be wearing vintage clothing, Emily."

Monique Lamartine gave an unexpected cackle of glee at that, something which startled her cat into taking off in the direction of Belvoir. "Catch him, Emily Jane," she wheezed. "Quick, before he disappears again."

"Let me," Lucas said, springing to his feet. "I need to stretch my legs a bit after spending the afternoon at the top of a ladder."

He needed to put a bit of distance between him and Emily, too. He'd made it plain that he needed time, but sitting so close that faint echoes of her perfume drifted past him every few seconds had left him dangerously susceptible to rushing things, particularly with her flaunting Bruce Anderson in his face.

She was trying to pressure him with one of the oldest tricks in the book, but he'd always prided himself on not being the jealous, possessive type. If he hoped to stick by that principle, however, he had a feeling he'd do well to keep himself very busy for the next little while. And if she kept up the pressure...well, then he wasn't sure if either of them was ready for a more final commitment.

CHAPTER EIGHT

ALTHOUGH Lucas had made it clear that his first priority was to rediscover the kind of man he was outside the parameters of his work, Emily hadn't expected that he'd act on it quite so soon. It began right then and there, however, with his chasing after Robespierre, and, given the cat's temperament, it ought to have qualified him for another citation of merit.

Even Monique was touched, though she did her best not to let it show. Beatrice, however, wasn't about to let her get away with that. "Admit it," she scolded, when Lucas returned covered with scratches and glory, and Robespierre tucked firmly under one arm. "You're a softie at heart where animals are concerned, Monique Lamartine, and you always have been."

"A softie?" Incensed, Monique glared at her. "Woman, you're senile!"

"Perhaps." Beatrice smiled reminiscently. "But I remember a summer morning many years ago when I went out to pick wild strawberries and found a fawn lying dead among the reeds by the river. Poor little thing had drowned, I believe, and I was beside myself for fear the grandchildren would come down and discover it—or worse yet that you might, Monique."

Monique looked suspicious. "How is it I never heard this story before, Beatrice?"

"We agreed not to tell you."

"We?" Emily asked, intrigued by this new snippet of family history.

"Your grandfather and I, darling."

128

The outrage Monique had shown when she was first a guest in the Flynn home and which had begun to diminish returned in full force, this time glazed in ice, but Beatrice appeared not to notice.

"Yes," she went on. "I met him on his way down to the river for his early morning swim. He did that every day of his life, if you remember."

"I scarcely need you to remind me of my husband's habits," Monique spat out. "I was married to him for nearly fifty years though I don't expect a little detail like that to trouble you."

Emily shot an inquiring glance at Lucas, who returned it with a faint shrug. From her grandmother's reaction, there was more to the story than met the eye, but he clearly had no more idea than she what it might be.

"He was a lovely man," Beatrice said softly, oblivious to Monique's quivering fury. "A sensitive man. He saw at once how upset I was, but even more he was concerned for you, Monique. You'd just lost another favorite pet—that aristocratic old Siamese that would eat only the finest canned salmon—and we agreed it would be cruel to add to your distress.

"So he dug a grave and I helped him bury that fawn. A few weeks later we planted a whole bed of calla lilies at the site and promised each other that we'd tell our secret to no one—though I don't think he'd mind my sharing it with you now.

"The flowers are still there and they always remind me of how kind he was, and how much he loved you. We were both very lucky women, Monique, when it came to husbands. Small wonder neither of us ever looked at another man when we lost the best."

She shook her head and blinked. "Well, that's enough of that! Who's ready for dinner? The fish market received a shipment of crab sent up fresh from San

Francisco just this morning, and I bought enough to feed an army."

Emily thought it sounded like a splendid idea and, judging from the way Lucas leapt to his feet, so did he. But Monique sat as if she were carved out of stone, staring sightlessly at the garden in front of her.

"Grand-mère?" Emily touched her shoulder. "Aren't you feeling well?"

Hearing the note of anxiety in her voice, Lucas came over. "Mrs. Lamartine, is something wrong?"

Monique swung a slow gaze from him to Beatrice and her eyes were black with pain. "I'm afraid there is," she said, "and it's much too late for anyone to do anything about it."

The doctor in Lucas took immediate charge. He checked her pulse, felt her cheek, the throbbing vein in her neck, and released the brake on her wheelchair.

"What is it?" Emily whispered, practically running to keep pace as he wheeled her grandmother swiftly back to the house.

"Her pulse is racing but don't ask me why. If I didn't know better, I'd say she'd just run a mile."

"Stop fussing, both of you," Monique ordered. "I'm not about to die and you won't find anything medically amiss. I shall be quite all right when I've had something to drink."

"I'll bring you a glass of water right away," Emily said, holding open the door to the sun room.

"I'm talking about cognac, Emily Jane. Save the water for another time when I'm more in command of myself."

"I'd like to examine you more thoroughly before you take any alcohol," Lucas said.

Monique heaved such a great sigh that Robespierre voiced his displeasure at being disturbed. "Young man," she decreed, soothing the cat with one hand and waving imperiously at Lucas with the other, "though it pleases me to see that you do indeed possess a modicum of professional responsibility after all, your concern is misdirected. I am not having a seizure, nor have I taken leave of my senses. Quite the opposite, if truth be known. Beatrice, I wish to speak with you alone as soon as it is convenient for you."

Not surprisingly, dinner was a somewhat subdued affair which for Emily descended into outright gloom when, before they had even finished the main course, the phone rang. "It's Tamara Golding for you, Lucas," Beatrice said. "Poor woman's terribly upset. Something about her little boy not being able to breathe and his doctor being away on holiday right now."

He went to the front hall to take the call and didn't have to offer a word on his return to the dining room for Emily to know what was coming. His expression said it all.

"You're rushing to the rescue," she said.

"The boy's an asthmatic, Emily. He needs help."

"Then perhaps he should be taken to the hospital."

He heard the cynicism in her voice, the peeved resignation she couldn't hide, and the look he brought to bear on her was frankly impatient. "Perhaps that's exactly what I intend to recommend. At the moment, however, his mother's in a state of panic and needs someone to take charge."

"Well, don't let me keep you in idle chitchat," Emily retorted with heavy sarcasm, ashamed to appear so unsympathetic but unable to shake the feeling that this was just another ruse on Tamara's part. What were the odds that by the time Lucas showed up on the doorstep the boy would have made a miraculous recovery?

For a moment, Lucas seemed torn. He even went so far as to lift his hand in a gesture that was almost pleading, then changed his mind and spun on his heel. "We'll talk when I get back," he said flatly, and a minute later the front door slammed behind him.

Fresh steamed crab lost its appeal after that, so Emily used Monique's request to speak privately to Beatrice as an excuse to escape to her own room. "I'd like to look through the clothes you mentioned, Mrs. Flynn," she said. "Try on a few and see if I can come up with something to wear to the winery event."

For a while she did just that, and became so engrossed that she forgot all about watching the clock for Lucas's return. There were some lovely things hanging in the wardrobe—romantic, Zelda Fitzgerald sort of clothing, with flowing scarves and wide-brimmed hats.

She considered and rejected a black lace shift trimmed with jet beads. It was meant for someone older and a little wider in the hips and shoulders. She fell in love with a two-piece affair in turquoise crepe with a cloche made of the same fine fabric, but the blouson top had a stained tear in it, as though it had been snagged on a rusty nail.

And then, when she'd just about given up on unearthing anything that would do, she found it: a floating dream of a dress in Nile green chiffon over ivory silk, with a dropped waist, full skirt and demurely high neckline. There were even shoes in matching ivory peau de soie—dainty little things with high heels and a strap across the instep. They fit as if they'd been made for her, and so did the dress.

She held up her hair in one hand, swirled in front of the full-length mirror, and decided that, come the night, she was going to give Tamara Golding a run for her money.

The minute Tamara's name came into her mind, however, the mood was broken. With a twinge of uneasiness, Emily noticed it was almost eleven o'clock. Lucas had been gone over three hours. When another had passed and there was still no sign of him, she threw on a robe and stole downstairs to the telephone in the front hall.

The grandmothers had long since finished their discussion and retired, so there was little chance of her being overheard as she dialed the number of April Water General Hospital and asked to be put through to Emergency.

"Yes," a nurse told her when she was connected, "Stuart Golding was brought in earlier this evening."

Emily cast a furtive glance over her shoulder, unbearably humiliated that she was allowing herself to behave so badly. "Um...how is he doing?"

"Very well," the anonymous voice replied. "We sent him home again about nine-thirty."

Too dismayed to be careful, Emily dropped the receiver with a clatter and decided she was going to be sick all over Beatrice's fine old Oriental rug. Just to reinforce the idea, the clock above the mantelpiece in the drawing room stroked out midnight.

What was keeping Lucas?

Clamping a hand to her mouth, she climbed the stairs. If this was what love did to a person, she thought, rushing to her bathroom, she clearly wasn't going to survive the experience.

The nausea passed but a headache—a real one this time, not just something conveniently manufactured— took hold. Dropping her robe in the middle of the floor, she eased herself down on the bed and willed her stomach to behave. Fifteen minutes later, she was back in the bathroom, and this time she really did lose her dinner.

Lucas came home just before two. She knew because she'd just hauled her aching body back to bed after her umpteenth visit to the toilet bowl, and saw the headlights of his car flash across her window as he drove into the garage at the side of the house.

She didn't hear him come up the stairs; it was difficult to hear anything over the pounding in her head.

*   *   *

The clock on the nightstand showed a quarter past nine when she awoke the next morning to sunlight streaking across the bed. Shielding her eyes, she sat up cautiously. Although the headache still nagged distantly, her stomach appeared to have recovered, and reacted quietly enough when she staggered to the bathroom to rinse her face in cold water.

She lifted her head and stared in horror at the pallid image reflected in the mirror above the vanity. She looked about as appealing as a wrung-out dishrag!

Even the effort of squeezing toothpaste on her brush left her trembling. Although it was not her normal morning preference, she would have sold her soul for a cup of tea, but the thought of navigating the stairs made it not worth the trouble.

She was perched on the edge of the tub, trying to decide if she really wanted a bath badly enough to run the risk of drowning from exhaustion, when a knock came at the bedroom door.

Twice she cleared her throat to call out. "Come in," she managed to croak on the third attempt.

"Heavenly days!" Beatrice exclaimed, flinging the door wide when she saw Emily tottering across the floor toward her. "Darling girl, whatever is the matter?"

She'd have shrugged except the effort required was more than she could spare. "I think I've come down with the flu," she managed feebly, "or else I ate something that disagreed with me."

"The crab!" Beatrice decided. "Dear Lord, where is Lucas when we need him?"

And she bustled away before Emily could stop her.

He showed up shortly thereafter, a distinctly sceptical expression on his face. "You're ill?" he inquired.

"It must have been the crab, Lucas," Beatrice said, bringing a damp cloth from the bathroom and dabbing at Emily's face. "When did the sickness come on, darling?"

"Last night," Emily said, feeling the room begin to spin again. "If you'll excuse me, I think I'd like to lie down."

Lucas placed a cool, professional palm on her forehead. "It's not likely to be the crab since we all ate it and no one else is suffering any ill effects," he said callously. "And you're not running a temperature. So what is it that's really bothering you, Emily Jane?"

He thought she was malingering! Begging for sympathy without due cause! And the fact that her stomach suddenly growled with hunger didn't do much for her credibility.

"She hardly ate a bite of dinner," Beatrice said unhelpfully. "Left the table as soon as you went out, now that I come to think of it, so perhaps you're right, Lucas. Perhaps it is the flu that's laid her so low."

"Or perhaps she's just plain hungry," he said, turning away in disgust. "Especially if my having to attend a medical emergency robbed her of her normally robust appetite."

"I threw up half the night," Emily informed his back, indignation lending her strength.

He yanked open the door. "Then I recommend dry toast and clear tea," he said shortly. "It's been known to work wonders on women suffering from the vapors."

"That's a wicked thing to say, Lucas!" Beatrice cried. "It was a foolish but unselfish thing she did, to suffer all night and not bother you."

"There wouldn't have been any point," Emily couldn't help saying. "By the time he came home, the worst was over."

He stopped in the doorway and flung her a look of such disgust that she shivered. "I'm flattered that you didn't let illness prevent your keeping tabs on me, Emily Jane. If you're not feeling better by this afternoon, let me know. I can always prescribe an antacid."

"He doesn't mean to be so abrupt with you," Beatrice consoled her after he'd left. "He's tired, that's all. Got in very late, I gather, but the Golding child is much better, thank the Lord."

I'm sure, Emily thought sourly. And I bet the widow Golding isn't doing too badly, either!

The damnable thing was, though, that Emily also felt much better as the day progressed. Enough to manage the recommended tea and toast for breakfast, and chicken broth with soda crackers for lunch.

"You're not to think of bringing me another meal in bed," she insisted when Beatrice caught her dressing for dinner. "I'm perfectly able to come down to the dining room."

"Why am I not surprised to see you?" Lucas sneered soon after when she slid into her seat at the table. "And looking so rosy and healthy, too! You've made an amazing recovery, Emily Jane."

"Of course she has," Monique said. "She's a Lamartine."

"I'm also wearing enough makeup to keep a cosmetic company in business for a year," Emily snapped, "but I don't expect you to believe me when I tell you that, Lucas."

"Why ever not?" he drawled. "Don't you always tell me the truth?"

His attitude made it perfectly clear that he thought she'd concocted the entire episode last night to wring a little attention from him, and she couldn't hide the hurt it caused her. All the progress they'd made, all the hopes and half-promises, seemed to evaporate before her eyes. He'd never taken her seriously. He never would.

To her horror, hunger and longing all mixed up with resentment and a kind of hopeless, angry adoration brought her to the edge of tears.

"Lucas!" his grandmother protested. "You're making Emily cry."

"Brute!" Monique spat.

Besieged on all sides, he glared at the three of them. "Oh, what the hell?" he growled, and, tossing aside his napkin, strode from the room.

Unable to stand the tense silence that followed his exit, Emily fled too. By then he'd reached the top of the stairs and was about to shut himself in his study.

"Just a minute, Lucas," she quavered, dashing away the tears still blurring her vision. "You and I have a few things to straighten out."

"You and I have nothing," he said bleakly, "nor are we ever likely to at this rate. I told you before, I won't be pressured into making a commitment I'm not sure either of us is ready for."

"*I*'m ready," she shot back. "It's—"

"Are you? I seem to remember telling you, the night before last, that I might sometimes put my work ahead of anything else, and you coming right back and saying you could live with that."

"Dropping everything to run over to Tamara Golding's every time she whimpers isn't your work! You're not her family doctor, or her son's."

"But I am still a doctor and I won't be held to account for decisions I make which I happen to think are right. I won't tolerate a curfew. And I won't let myself be manipulated by a woman who acts like a child every time she doesn't get her own way."

Bright red rage filmed Emily's eyes, scorching any remnant of tears into oblivion. "But you don't mind being manipulated by a woman who uses an innocent child to get what she wants. Tell me, Lucas, what makes Tamara's behavior so much more acceptable than mine? How is it you're able to spare her understanding and kindness, but dole them out to me in such meager amounts?"

"She wasn't being manipulative. Her son had a very bad asthma attack and she was terrified. With good reason, I might add. The last time that happened, the boy wound up on a ventilator in ICU for three days.''

"Is that why you stayed by her side half the night, even though the emergency was over hours earlier?''

"How do you know that, Emily Jane?''

She'd reached the top of the stairs and stood close enough to touch him but suddenly she wished she'd stayed at the table and kept her mouth shut. "Never mind,'' she said, backing away.

His hand shot out and clamped around her arm. "I said, how do you know that, Emily Jane?''

So often since they'd met again he'd behaved as if he'd died out there in Africa, and she'd sometimes thought that if all that was left was a shell of the man he used to be it might have been better if he had. But she saw now that the last vestige of that monastic calm was gone, shattered by a fury that made her flinch.

"What else could have kept you away so long?'' she temporized, unable to repress the tremor in her voice.

He gave a little jerk and brought her up so close that she could feel the buckle of his belt stabbing into her. "You're lying again, Emily.''

"Oh, all right!'' she cried, squirming under his scrutiny. "I phoned the hospital and they told me.''

"You checked up on me?''

"Yes, I checked up on you,'' she wailed, a fresh spate of tears rolling down her face. "The same way you checked up on me the night I went for a stroll with Bruce.''

He held her close to him a second longer. Close enough to kiss her—and oh, she wanted him to kiss her! Wanted him to let that iron grip subside into a caress, to slide his arms around her and tell her that she was silly to be so insecure and that he'd never look at another woman as long as he had her.

Instead, he let her go, the way she might have dropped a hot saucepan lid. "I have no use for jealousy,'' he said. "No matter how you look at it, it's ugly and insulting. Worse, it's destructive. Only a fool would try to build a relationship on it."

And, swinging around, he strode into his study and let the door slam shut in her face.

That was the last Emily saw of Lucas for the remainder of the week. Faced as she was with the task of hiring short-term staff and ordering supplies for the banquet, her own days were too full for her to spare the time to monitor his comings and goings. Still, she couldn't help noticing, when she went out each morning to the car that Beatrice had kindly lent her, that the other half of the garage where Lucas normally kept his station wagon stood empty.

"You're working much too hard, *ma chère,*" Monique scolded, when Emily showed up late for dinner on the third day. "I hope Madame Golding is suitably appreciative."

"Beyond signing a contract the first morning, I've scarcely seen her," Emily said. "She hasn't once set foot in the kitchen area. If she has a question that needs answering, or some matter that needs attention, she sends for me."

"Sends for you?"

"That's right, Grand-mère, and frankly I prefer it that way. I couldn't stand having her underfoot all the time, checking to make sure I know what I'm doing. She remains in her executive office and I stick to the kitchen where she undoubtedly feels I belong."

"Tell us what we'll be eating, Emily, darling," Beatrice wheedled.

"I've kept it pretty plain. Beef tenderloin, and local fruit and vegetables—the kind of things that most people enjoy. I'll wait until I'm set up in my own establishment with a permanent staff before I branch out into more exotic menus."

Beatrice nodded. "The men will be pleased. It's been my experience that they prefer plain food."

"Speaking of men," Emily said, trying to sound only marginally interested, "where's Lucas these days? Or is he avoiding me?"

"Of course he's not, darling! He's up to his neck in some important experiment at the lab and staying in the city till he's finished. He does that occasionally when things get hectic."

"I see." Emily nodded, then added with feigned nonchalance, "Will he be too busy to attend the banquet?"

"Heavens, no! When he phoned yesterday, he mentioned that he'd spoken to Tamara and would be back no later than noon on Saturday. Plenty of time for him to get out of his lab coat and into his dinner suit."

Emily digested that item of news with difficulty. So he'd had time to talk to Tamara, but not found a minute to let her know he was going to be in the city for a few days. It was enough to sour anyone's hopes!

She said as much to Monique on the Friday. "I half dread tomorrow night, Grand-mère."

"I'd have thought you'd be looking forward to it. It's your chance to dazzle the entire community. After this, I shouldn't expect you'll have any trouble picking up clients, Emily Jane."

"Perhaps, but...well, with Tamara Golding flaunting herself...." Emily lifted her shoulders in mute disgust.

"Why do you care how she chooses to behave?" her grandmother asked. "You don't normally concern yourself over such trivial matters."

Emily had the grace to look embarrassed.

"I see," Monique observed, "that 'normal' doesn't apply in this case. You perceive her as a threat, do you, Emily Jane? Not to the success of your professional undertaking, but as someone who might come between you and Lucas Flynn?"

"Yes," Emily said, and, when her grandmother went to interrupt, insisted, "I know I'm not mistaken, Grand-mère. A woman in love always senses when someone else is after her man, don't you think?"

"Not always," Monique said, somewhat to Emily's surprise. "Things aren't always as they seem, ma chère. Sometimes appearances can be deceiving."

"But she's so obvious! She as good as told me to back off. Rubbed my nose in the fact that he'd accepted an invitation to sit at her table tomorrow night and that, even if I did manage to get my act together well enough to spend part of the time as a guest, I needn't expect there'd be room there for me."

"There's nothing you can do about that, Emily Jane. It's up to Lucas to tell her he's not interested, if that is indeed the case."

"And I should sit back and do nothing, the way I did before, and watch another woman walk off with him?"

"For a relationship to stand any chance at all, there are two things a woman must learn to do, Emily Jane. One is to accept the fact that you cannot force feelings. Either they're there or they're not. The other is to learn to trust. There's no telling the damage done by a lack of trust."

"How can I trust him when all Tamara Golding has to do is crook her little finger and he races to be by her side?"

Monique swiveled her chair to face the window that looked out on the orchard at the side of the house. Beyond it rose the belt of cypress trees that separated the property from Belvoir.

"Listen to me, Emily Jane," she said. "For years I believed your grandfather was having an affair with Beatrice. Yes, you might well gasp like that, but I thought I had good cause.

"Early one morning I happened to look out of my bedroom window and I saw them together. He had his

arm around her and suddenly, as if he could feel my
gaze on him, he looked back at the house, then hurried
her out of sight among those trees over there.

"It was a long time before they came back again, and
when they did she was weeping. He held her in his arms
and she leaned against him and sobbed her heart out,
the way a woman does when something has hurt her
deeply. Eventually, he put her from him and gave her a
little push, as though to say, 'It's over. Go home to your
husband.'"

"Beatrice and Grand-père?" Emily said in hushed
disbelief. "But you and he always seemed so happy
together, so in tune with each other!"

"We were," Monique said. "That is why I waited for
him to come to me and tell me what it was I'd witnessed,
because I was sure there must be an explanation beyond
the obvious. But he never did, although I gave him the
opportunity over and over again. He never referred to
seeing Beatrice that day and when I came right out and
asked him what had kept him so long past the time he
usually was gone for his morning swim he made up some
story about not realizing how late it was."

"Why didn't you confront him?"

"Because I loved him and was afraid of losing him.
I should have known better, of course, because by then
we'd been married long enough to have grandchildren
running about the place and he'd never once given me
reason to doubt him in all that time. But I never set foot
in Beatrice Flynn's house again and I made sure she never
set foot in mine. Two years later, your grandfather was
dead, but they weren't happy years, Emily Jane. What
had happened put such strain between us and he didn't
understand how or why."

She sighed and a tear rolled down her cheek. Emily
was appalled. In all the years of her growing up she'd
never seen her grandmother cry. "You should have talked
to him, Grand-mère. Brought it all out into the open."

"Yes," Monique said as another tear slipped down her face. "Instead I waited twenty-one years for an explanation, and found out the other day that I'd punished two people who meant the whole world to me. And why? Because they loved me enough to want to protect me from hurt."

"Oh, Grand-mère, it was all about the fawn!" Emily put her arms around the thin, stooped shoulders. "How sad!"

"How wicked," Monique declared, some of the starch returning to her voice, "to have wasted all that time. Don't make the same mistake with Lucas, Emily Jane. If you think you can make a life with this man, don't spoil it with doubt and jealousy."

"Lucas as good as said the same thing the night after he went rushing over to help Tamara's son."

"He was right to do so. Jealousy can undermine even the strongest of bonds."

Emily sighed unhappily. "Before that night, he and I talked and it seemed as though there was a chance for us. He asked me to give him time to be sure that we both wanted the same thing, and I said I would. I meant it at the time, but now...I don't know. When I was eighteen, I was prepared to wait for him for ever; at thirty I'm not so naive as to think that's possible."

"*Do* you love him?"

That, at least, was simple to answer. "Yes," Emily said. "I have always loved him and I always will. But I'm afraid he might not feel the same way about me."

"Lucas Flynn is strong-willed, just as his grandfather was, and he won't be coerced. Try to rush him and you'll lose him." Monique spun the chair back to face her and, taking her hand, chafed it gently with her own. "I hope he deserves your love, Emily Jane, but the only way you'll find out for sure is to give him the freedom to walk away from it."

* * *

Advice didn't come much better than that, Emily decided early the next evening as she eased her toes into sheer silk stockings the color of morning mist. And in another two hours she'd have the chance to show whether or not she was equal to the task of following it.

She'd spent the day at the winery, supervising the final details for the evening ahead. Among the hastily assembled staff of twelve whom she'd hired, she'd been lucky enough to find two women who'd worked for years in the hotel business. At half past five, with everything ready except for the finishing touches, she'd felt confident enough to leave things in their hands while she went back to Roscommon to dress.

Bruce had arranged for a limousine to collect her and the grandmothers and that afternoon had had corsages delivered to the house. "A lovely man he is, to be sure," Beatrice had sighed happily, showing off her purple orchids to Emily when she'd arrived home.

"But not the right man, *hélas!*" Monique had murmured, inhaling the delicate fragrance of her tea roses.

For Emily he had ordered gardenias, two perfect, exquisite blooms which she now pinned in the upswept coils of her hair. Around her neck she wore the Lamartine pearls which her grandmother had lent her for the evening. They and the flowers were all the accessories the dress required.

"Oh!" Bruce said with great feeling, when she came downstairs just before seven o'clock.

If Emily hadn't been sure what to make of that, Beatrice's response left her in little doubt that she'd chosen her outfit well. "You look lovely, Emily, darling, just lovely!" she cried. "You'll outshine every other woman there, no doubt about it."

Monique, who'd graduated from the wheelchair to her cane for the evening, gave her a peck on the cheek and whispered, "And you will have fun tonight. Don't spoil the whole effect by languishing in a corner because he's dancing with someone else, Emily Jane, or you might as well show up in sackcloth and remain hidden in the kitchen.''

Lucas couldn't offer his comments because he'd left just after six to pick up Tamara Golding and drive her to the winery early enough for her to be on hand to greet the rest of the guests.

Just as well, Emily thought wryly. In light of his mood at their last meeting, he'd probably have told her she looked like something Robespierre had caught floating in the river.

CHAPTER NINE

THE April Valley Winery was housed in a stone building that looked very much like a French château and was, in fact, a magnificent private residence as well as an operating wine-making establishment. Its great entrance hall, floored in marble, was overflowing with flowers, music and people by the time the limousine rolled to a stop at its massive front doors.

The first person Emily recognized was Tamara. She would have been hard to miss in a crowd of thousands, let alone the couple of hundred people present that night. Clothed from head to foot in gleaming gold lamé, she looked, Emily decided uncharitably, like a curvaceous Egyptian mummy.

She was also at her corporate best. "How very nice that you got the potatoes peeled in time to join us," she murmured to the gardenia behind Emily's right ear. "Do help yourself to champagne—unless, of course, you feel you must rush away to the kitchen."

Emily was very glad that Bruce stood at her elbow. He might not be the man of her heart but there was no denying that he was a sight worth seeing in black tie and dinner jacket. Like Lucas, he had shoulders that begged to show off fine tailoring. Even Tamara spared him a second glance.

Leaving the grandmothers in his care, Emily excused herself and did exactly as Tamara had suggested, threading her way among the throng of guests to the wide passage at the back of the hall that led to the kitchens.

As she had expected, everything there was running like clockwork, and after a quick check with the staff and an assurance that she'd be back again before the final countdown she returned to the pre-dinner reception. Bruce had temporarily disappeared, but Lucas stood chatting with Beatrice and Monique.

"Some shindig," he muttered, snagging a glass of champagne from the tray of a passing waiter and handing it to Emily. "They never had do's like this here when I was growing up."

"Indeed not," Monique said. "You were right, Beatrice, in saying that the custom started some five years back. And there weren't enough chairs then either, as I recall."

"Darling," Beatrice cried, slipping her arm through Monique's, "is your poor knee bothering you? Shall we find a place to sit?"

"Is something going on that I'm not aware of?" Lucas asked, staring after them in blank amazement as they wove a determined path through the crowd. "Shouldn't your grandmother be tripping up mine with her cane about now?"

Emily had a hard time answering. The sight of him in formal attire took her breath away, and that, added to what felt suspiciously like the beginnings of a cold, left her voice trapped somewhere at the back of her throat.

It wasn't enough to say he looked handsome. Devastatingly magnificent, perhaps, or overwhelmingly masculine. But most of all he looked sexy. From the top of his shining black hair to the tips of his gleaming black shoes, he epitomized male sexuality on the loose, and Emily felt ready to claw out the eyes of any woman who came within six feet of him.

She blinked, belatedly recalling her grandmother's advice. Forcing herself not to devour him with her gaze, she swallowed to relieve her dry throat and said, "They

had a long chat the other night and seem to have sorted
out their differences. Perhaps we should try to do the
same."

His gaze roamed her face searchingly, perhaps even
entreatingly. "Do you think that's possible, Emily?"

"Why not?" she said with a great show of airy confidence even though, inside, what she really wanted to
do was fall down, fling her arms around his knees and
beg him, please, not to look at another woman ever again
for as long as he lived. "We're two civilized adults, after
all, and this is a *very* pleasant way to spend an evening.
I must remember to thank Tamara for letting me be a
part of it."

He looked rather suspicious at that, which led Emily
to wonder if she wasn't laying it on a bit too thick.
"Speaking of Tamara..." he began.

With profound relief, Emily saw Bruce weaving his
way back to her through the press of bodies just in time
to spare her having to pretend an interest in the one
person she'd as soon forget.

"They're asking people to find their dinner tables,
Emily," he said. "I got your grandmother and Mrs.
Flynn settled and thought perhaps you'd like to get
seated, too."

"Go on without me, Bruce," she said. "I'll make one
last run to the kitchen before I join you. I dare say I'll
see you later, Lucas. Good luck with your speech."

"Speech?" he echoed, the beginnings of a scowl
marring the perfection of his brow.

She gave a vague little wave of the hand. "Of thanks.
For the honor being conferred on you this evening." And
by dint of extraordinary self-control she managed to sway
away without dragging her feet or flinging longing gazes
at him over her chiffon-draped shoulder.

In the kitchen, the staff stood ready to deliver the first
course. Emily ran a practiced eye over the plates, noted
that the garnishes had been arranged exactly as she'd

specified, checked the ovens containing the entrées, and
smiled her approval. "Allow another five minutes for
late arrivals to get seated, then start serving the appe-
tizers. I'll pop back here in between courses to lend a
hand, and I'm at the table to the right as you come into
the dining hall, if you need me at any other time."

The banquet room was almost as impressive as the
entrance hall, with fourteen highly polished chandeliers
reflecting light on the silver and crystal table settings.
At one end of the floor, on a raised platform banked
with lilies and roses, stood a podium with a micro-
phone—the place, no doubt, where the citations of merit
would be presented.

Lucas sat four tables removed from Emily's, with his
back toward her. There was no missing the twinkling of
Tamara's dress in the light of the chandeliers as she
shimmied into the chair beside him; no mistaking the
way she leaned toward him, all smiles and cleavage.

Aware of Monique's mindful gaze, and of Bruce, who
was about as charming and attentive an escort as any
woman could wish for, Emily made a concerted effort
to enjoy herself when she wasn't darting back and forth
to the kitchen. She nibbled at the smoked salmon, the
artichokes, the beef Wellington, and found them superb.
Judged the strawberry meringues and sherbet flawless.
And, when her contribution to the success of the evening
finally wound down, she frankly relished the fine *di-
gestif* without which she wasn't sure she could have endured watching Tamara play handmaiden to Paolo
Savardi, the owner of the winery, as he presented the
evening's honorees with their engraved plaques.

Lucas was the last to be called up. Like Bruce, he made
his acknowledgement short and to the point and afterward would have followed the example of his pre-
decessors and simply walked across the dais and taken
his seat at the table again. But Tamara, whose taxing
job it had been to hand each plaque to her employer as

its recipient's name was announced, caught Lucas by the hand as he made to pass by her and planted a kiss full on his mouth.

She might as well have slapped a "SOLD" sign on his lapel.

Amid the applause, Emily sat in frozen dismay, the strawberry meringue dessert thumping like lead to the pit of her stomach.

"Well," Beatrice observed rather dubiously as the clapping died down, "that was a bit of a surprise, don't you think?"

"Indeed." Monique sat like a duchess, the look she sent skating across the table to Emily suggesting that she find the self-possession to do likewise. "Lucas looked quite taken aback. Unpleasantly so, one might almost say."

"Just a little embarrassed, perhaps," Emily remarked gamely, then dropped her serviette and pushed herself away from the table. "Will you all excuse me one last time? I'd like to make sure things are running smoothly at the back and thank my staff again for a job well done."

When she returned, dancing had begun in the great hall. Candlelight flickered from wall sconces, an orchestra played in the gallery above, and the whole scene might have been plucked from a page of European history had the parking lot beyond the illuminated gardens been filled with horse-drawn carriages instead of exotic Porsches and Mercedes.

Bruce was not the only man anxious to partner Emily. Paolo Savardi, an urbane, intelligent man in his midforties, sought her out more than once, too, and heaped praise on her for the wonderful meal she'd managed to create at such short notice. "Care to dance—again?" he smiled, coming back for the third time.

And dance she did, until her feet were ready to drop off and her lungs were fit to burst, spinning around the marble floor with her chiffon floating around her like a cloud.

Somewhere in the hall, Lucas was dancing too, but she refused to let her gaze seek him out. Instead she smiled and laughed and flirted harmlessly with Bruce and Paolo, felt her cheeks grow flushed and her head begin ever so delicately to throb and her breathing become a little labored.

"More champagne, Emily?" Paolo inquired, some time between eleven and midnight.

He offered her a crystal flute filled with sparkling gold liquid, and she saw that the backs of his broad, strong hands were covered with springy dark hair. He wore a diamond-studded gold Rolex watch on his wrist and gold studs in his shirt and at his cuffs.

Fingering the pearls at her neck, she debated the offer for a moment, then reached out to take the tulip-shaped glass. "Lovely," she murmured.

As it would have been, had she been allowed to take a sip, because her throat felt a little like sandpaper, probably from all the exertion she'd expended on the dance floor. But then another hand intervened, lean and long-fingered, tanned and elegant. No gold watch, no gold studs, and not much hair.

"You don't need that," Lucas said, his voice a whipcord of disapproval, and Emily looked up to find his beautiful azure eyes boring into her, full of fire and fury.

"Hello, Lucas," she said, a trifle hoarsely. "Where's Tamarakins?"

"Dancing," he said shortly. "Why don't we do the same?"

As if he needed to ask! As if she hadn't waited all night to feel his arms around her and his thighs nudging hers as he swept her around the room, away from Bruce, away from Paolo Savardi.

Away from everybody. Because suddenly they were
outside and the night air was cooling her flushed face
and the stars were shining down discreetly, and he was
half dragging her away from the music and gaiety of the
great hall and into the shadows of the garden.

"Where are you taking me?" she murmured, her arm
still looped around his shoulder.

"I'm going to dump you head-first in the fish pond,"
he said, "and hope that it sobers you up."

"But I'm not drunk, Lucas." Nor was she. She'd had
no more than three or four glasses of wine all evening
long. Whatever was making her feel so strangely light-
headed and unable to breathe had nothing to do with
alcohol.

"I hope you are," he practically snarled. "Because
I'd hate to think you'd act like such a fool if you
weren't."

"Was I acting like a fool?" she said, sinking onto a
stone bench and wishing she could draw a breath deep
enough to fill her beleaguered lungs.

He hauled her to her feet. "What else would you call
letting that lech paw you in full view of his wife and
every other person in the room?"

Her high heels caught in the raked gravel of the path,
sending her stumbling against him. "But Lucas, Bruce
isn't married and he isn't a lech," she protested, clutching
at his lapel.

Even with just the stars to illuminate his face, she saw
the rage that contoured his features into stone. "The
games and nonsense never stop with you, do they, Emily?
You know damn well that I'm not referring to Bruce
Anderson."

She realized then what it was that had fueled his fury,
and her heart did a joyful little song and dance behind
her ribs. "Lucas!" she breathed. "You're jealous! Of
Paolo Savardi, of all people!"

For one astonished moment, she thought he was going to slap her. He reared back and lifted his hand, but then she saw that all the anger had seeped out of him and that a different kind of torment flared in his eyes.

"When are *you* going to stop all this nonsense and kiss me, Lucas?" she whispered.

And that was all it took. He wove his fingers into the coils of hair piled high on her head, wrapped his other arm firmly around her waist to bring her hard up against him, and slanted his mouth across hers.

He consumed her soul with that kiss. He took her heart and branded it his for the rest of time. He let loose a hunger in both of them that was tired of being patient, sick to death of waiting until other things had sorted themselves out. Because, when all was said and done, nothing else but this mattered.

At least, that was the way it seemed to her, and she thought he felt the same way. Because when she took his hand and brought it to her breast he didn't try to stop her. He slid his palm over the filmy chiffon and up to that chastely high neckline until he found the row of hooks and eyes that held it closed at her nape.

His nimble doctor's fingers went to work and suddenly the Lamartine pearls lay cool against her bare skin. He traced a row of short, swift kisses down her throat and then his mouth was hot and damp on her nipple, inciting it to aching vibrancy beneath its covering of fine lace.

She drew in a constricted breath, buried her face in his thick hair, and begged him with small, incoherent pleas not to let anything break the magic. But the colored lanterns strung through the trees invited anyone of a mind to do so to wander at will through the garden. Other guests could come upon them at any moment, something of which she was made acutely aware as voices not twenty yards away penetrated her haze of pleasure.

Lucas heard them too. Spinning her around, he shielded her with the breadth of his shoulders and hastily pulled her dress back into place. She knew, with wrenching futility, that this would be all the excuse he would need to hark back to that old familiar theme of the time and the place not being right, and she couldn't bear it.

"No," she begged, her hands everywhere on him. "No, I won't let you do this to us again."

"What the hell, Emily...?" he muttered raggedly. "Isn't it enough that you put on a floor show inside, without giving an encore out here as well?"

But it was just talk—a lie that his body didn't believe for a moment. He strained against her, hard and heavy with desire beneath the snug fit of his trousers, and nothing he might say or do could deny the fact.

"Come with me," she cajoled, her fingers inciting him with delicate, deliberate intent.

Beyond the musical splash of the fountain in the fish pond, a path veered off. With all the guile at her command, she lured him down that dark, narrow route, tormenting him every step of the way, scattering kisses over his mouth, brushing against him seductively, then twisting away, ephemeral as a shadow, knowing that he would follow wherever she led.

They came out at the back of the parking lot. No romantic lanterns here to invite intrusion. No velvet stretch of lawn to cushion bodies driven past rectitude to blind, consuming passion. Just the sleek, dormant shapes of automobiles, their metal sheaths smooth and cool against heated flesh, their windows blank and unseeing.

She heard his indrawn breath and knew exactly the torture it exacted. Weren't her own lungs fighting just as hard to fuel her with the strength to put the seal of completion on something that had started years ago and never been resolved?

She drew him to her again, angled herself against him. As if she'd been fashioned for no other man but him, her body fit, each curve finding its appointed niche.

The Nile-green chiffon drifted high, the elastic waist of her silk panties slid down past her hips. A delicate rasp cut through the night, that of a metal zipper sliding open. And suddenly he was against her, molten velvet fortified with steel, urgent, demanding, irresistible.

All lustrous, silken heat, she offered herself, and the waiting was over. He braced himself with one hand against the roof of the nearest car, pinned her against the door with the other. She felt herself opening, dissolving, swelling, filling with love and hunger and pleasure. Filling with him.

He kissed her again. Slid his mouth along her jaw, swirled his tongue over the outer shell of her ear, and let it dance a moist duet with the surging power of his thrusts.

It had been eleven years since they'd shared such intimacy but it might have been just yesterday. He knew when she climbed that last steep ascent and, though it seemed almost to destroy him, he slowed his pace and waited for her.

Clawing at the fine black wool of his dinner jacket, she reached the peak. With a great groan of release, he supported her as they tumbled headlong down the other side. Held her close as she melted around him, battered and exhausted.

The magnificence of it all reduced her to tears. They streamed down her face, turning the stars into a million prisms of dazzling light. Too soon, his breathing slowed, though hers continued to fight painfully for release. "Oh, Lucas...!" she sighed, almost strangling herself on the words. "How I've longed to have you make love to me again!"

He was so unkind, so cold that it was difficult to believe he'd filled her with the liquid heat of his passion mere seconds before. "And what has it proved," he asked wearily, pushing away from her to lean against the side of the car, "beyond the fact that we both keep our brains in our pants?"

A draft of cool air flowed over her, chilling the trickle of moisture seeping down her thigh. "Don't turn away from me like that, Lucas," she said in a small, hurt voice. "I love you!"

"Yeah?" He yanked his clothing into order, self-disgust evident in every taut line of him. "And how many men have heard you say that, Emily?"

"Just two," she said, tugging her skirt down around her legs again, where it properly belonged, and fighting to draw another breath. The air was so close suddenly, so full of humidity that her lungs seemed to be drowning in it. "But I only told the truth with one, and he wasn't the man I was married to."

Dismissing the admission, Lucas turned away. As if the gates of heaven were about to close against her, she reached for him, misjudging the distance and catching only the cuff of his jacket. "Where are you going?" she whimpered, the tears gurgling in her throat.

"Back to my partner for the evening," he said. "Unless, of course, there's something more I can do for you?"

The words slashed her pride to ribbons and let the anguish come flooding out. "You could tell me that this time you knew what you were doing," she said brokenly. "That I wasn't some figment of a dream or a case of mistaken identity. You could tell me that making love to me matters more to you than dancing attendance on Tamara Golding. Just once, Lucas, you could say to hell with what you think you ought to do, and follow your instincts instead."

"Anything else?" he inquired, the emotional distance between them yawning wider with every word.

"You could tell me you love me," she whimpered pitifully.

He waited a long time before replying, the seconds strung out one after the other with his unspoken admission hovering between them.

Say it, she begged silently. Please, my darling man, just say the words. The world won't come to an end.

"And you could be pregnant," he said. "Don't ask me to indulge your romantic yearnings when all I can think of is that I just behaved like a self-indulgent, uncontrolled fool—again."

She'd long ago adjusted to the idea that she'd never have babies, but love, happy ever after? Were they beyond reach, too?

Apparently they were.

"You've got this lame-brained notion that you're going to save my soul whether or not I want you to," Lucas said, spitting the words out like bullets. "But what if I don't have a soul worth saving, Emily Jane? What if I don't need a guardian angel to set me on the right path?"

Perhaps passion couldn't survive the sort of crushing disappointment that lanced her then, but anger possessed an amazing ability to retaliate. "And what if I'm nothing but a fool to fall in love with an ignorant, passive clod who turned off the main switch years ago and ended up about as interesting as a brain-dead lemming?" she cried.

"You're finally getting the message," Lucas said. "Whatever took you so long?"

She stared at him, so full of hopeless, helpless longing that the misery of it threatened to suffocate her. "I think..." she coughed a little, and was aware of a faint, alarming rattle deep in her chest "...we've said enough. I'd like to go home now, if you don't mind. I'm really not feeling very well, Lucas."

It was something of an understatement. In fact, she felt very strange.

"Of course you're not," he jeered, with patent disbelief. "You never are when things don't go your way. What's it going to be this time? Headache? Upset stomach? Double pneumonia?"

His voice came to her in waves, sometimes washing over her, other times echoing from afar. When, instead of answering, she turned and leaned against the car for support, he gave a snort of weary disgust. "Save it, Emily Jane! It's not going to work with me, though you might have better luck with good old Bruce."

Too defeated to try any more and too exhausted to care, she waited until he'd disappeared, then stumbled away into the concealing darkness.

Bruce was just coming to look for her when she showed up at the big front door. "I was beginning to worry about you," he said. "Where have you been?"

"To hell," she croaked. "Please take me home, Bruce. I think I'm coming down with something."

He didn't ask questions or make snide remarks about how much she'd had to drink. He didn't chastise her for abandoning him, or accuse her of behaving badly with other women's husbands. He simply said, "You've pushed yourself too hard and you're worn out," then took charge with a minimum of fuss and more kindness and concern than she had any right to expect.

He rounded up the grandmothers and ushered them out to the waiting limousine. He said he hoped she'd feel better by the morning and asked her please to call him if there was anything he could do for her.

She sank into the limousine's plush leather seat and rested her aching head against the cool glass of the window at her side, and wondered why he couldn't be the right man for her.

* * *

The damned bow tie had been choking Lucas all evening. Cursing, he flung it across his room, tore off his stiffly starched shirt, tossed his dinner suit to the back of his clothes closet. And still her perfume clung to him.

Ashamed, he slumped on the side of the bed and sank his head in his hands. How could he have let himself make such a colossal, undignified mess of things?

He'd taken her up against the side of a car, for crying out loud, with no more finesse or tenderness than a stallion attacking a brood mare! His lovely, gracious Emily, for whom the evening had been a social and professional triumph, had ended the night in tears because he hadn't the wit or decency to keep a rein on his libido.

He was within spitting distance of forty. What the blazes had he been thinking of, behaving like such an ass? What was it about her that induced him to such madness that living for the moment, wildly, irresponsibly, became the most overriding need in his universe?

Living?

He wiped his palms down his face and stifled a groan. He had died in her arms, found heaven buried inside her. Why hadn't he told her that, instead of turning away from her?

He knew why.

Somehow, through all the loss and failure she had known, she'd retained that quality of innocence and absolute shining belief in love and happy endings that she'd had as a girl. And he was terrified of disappointing her—scared to death that, one day, she'd look at him and he'd see that the light had gone out in her eyes.

It wasn't a question of whether or not he loved her, it was a question of whether his kind of love would be enough. He wasn't an easy man, he knew. He was professionally driven and, because of it, often isolated. He and Sydney had been alike in that respect, which was perhaps why their partnership had survived.

Emily wasn't like Sydney, though. She would demand more, and he'd already disappointed her once. What if he disappointed her again by giving so much to his research that not enough was left over to make her happy?

The bottom line was, she'd be better off with a nice, uncomplicated guy like Bruce Anderson, with someone who left his work behind at the end of the day and threw himself wholeheartedly into the other half of his life—that which revolved around home and family. Yet the thought of Anderson or any other man laying claim to her left Lucas blind with rage and jealousy.

Disgusted all over again with his dog-in-the-manger attitude, he strode to the door, down the stairs and out of the house. He couldn't go on like this. For both their sakes, he had to make up his mind.

Faint starlight was reflected on the river rolling black and smooth as oil past the bottom of the garden. He stood poised for a moment on the end of the diving pier, then sliced into the water. Let it close over his head and sweep him out into center stream where the current ran strong.

Let it sift through the indecision and uncertainty clouding his mind until there was nothing left but the truth that had lain hidden in his heart all along.

Emily dreamed that night that she was drowning. The water filled her lungs, choking the life out of her. Everything turned red and a great rushing noise roared in her ears. Struggle though she might, she could not surface long enough to draw breath into her failing body. The weeds had tangled too thoroughly around her legs, dragging her down.

Lucas was on the shore but he didn't see her. He was dancing with Tamara Golding. She wore a long white gown and he was in tails, even though, from the position of the sun and the way the mist floated around their ankles, it had to be early morning.

Then Tamara turned around and looked at the river. Laughing, she tossed a bouquet of flowers onto the water. A bridal bouquet. It came to rest right above where Emily sank to the bottom for the last time....

When Lucas went downstairs the next morning, the grandmothers had already finished breakfast. However, Emily's place was still set, so he assumed he wasn't the only one who'd slept late.

"Good morning." Only Monique Lamartine could weigh such a simple greeting with so much hidden meaning.

What did she expect him to reply? That it was a whole hell of a lot better than the night before? "Good morning," he said.

"Had a nice rest last night, did you, Lucas?" Bea asked, filling his coffee cup.

"Excellent. Better than I have in years."

"Only a clear conscience will do that for a person," Monique said ominously.

Trust her to try to cast a pall over the day by reminding him of last night's folly just when he'd begun to feel better about things! His midnight swim had achieved exactly what he'd hoped for and he finally felt that he had a handle on a way to work things out with Emily.

Today he planned to take her for a drive. A few miles north of where the April river emptied into the Pacific, a small hotel stood at the top of the cliffs, with a view from the dining terrace that spread for miles in every direction.

Perhaps there, away from the curious eyes and attentive ears roaming loose at Roscommon, he could apologize to her and try to make her understand that it wasn't so much her he had rejected last night as himself. If she could accept that and the fact that he was still feeling his way into a future not nearly as well defined as he'd like it to be, perhaps they could behave like the civilized adults she'd claimed they were and go about discovering the full potential of their relationship the way normal people did, with dinner dates, movies, the odd show in San Francisco, a weekend away on occasion.

The point was, they needed to get to know each other as they were now, instead of relying on the memory of how they used to be, find out at a slow and easy pace the other dimensions on which they hoped to build a future, beyond the sexual magnetism that neither seemed able to withstand.

"I have a batch of batter waiting by the stove, Lucas," Bea said, obviously mistaking his silence for raging hunger. "I'll go and see how much longer Emily's likely to be, then get started cooking up a plate of hot cakes."

The silence, when she left the room, fairly zinged with tension. "Did you enjoy yourself last night, Mrs. Lamartine?" he asked, when he could stand it no more.

"Very much, thank you."

"Your knee wasn't too painful?"

"No."

"That's good." He drummed his fingers on the table. "I see you're not in your wheelchair this morning either. Maybe you're not going to need it as long as you'd expected."

She fixed him with the sharp black stare of a schoolmarm inspecting an intellectually subnormal student. "Did you enjoy *yourself* last night, Lucas?"

"I...er...yes, in a way, though that sort of affair isn't really my idea of a good time."

"Was that why you spoilt the evening for my granddaughter? Because she was having fun and you weren't?"

"Did she say I spoiled the evening for her, Mrs. Lamartine?" he said, tossing the conversational ball back into her court. She was going to have to take a much more subtle approach than that if she sincerely expected to worm information out of him.

Monique Lamartine squared her frail old shoulders obstinately. "She was full of life and laughter until you asked her to dance," she said, then let a pregnant pause spin out before adding pointedly, "The next time I saw her, she was as crushed as the gardenias in her hair, and so, come to that, was her gown."

He almost choked on his coffee. Why didn't she just come right out and ask if he'd managed to keep his pants done up? "Gardenias are very fragile flowers, I believe," he said, recovering his composure with difficulty.

"As is my granddaughter, Lucas Flynn, and while you were too young and foolish to recognize that fact eleven years ago I had hoped you'd gained the maturity and wisdom to recognize it now."

Uncertain how to respond to that without condemning himself further, he expelled a long breath and stared out of the window. When was someone going to rescue him from this patrician barracuda?

Bea did, soon after. The door opened and she came into the room. But her step had lost its vigor and her voice, when she spoke, trembled with agitation. "Lucas...!" she began, one fist pressed to her chest.

"For God's sake, Gran!" Alarmed to see her looking so ashen, he shoved back his chair and sprang to his feet, all manner of fears crowding his mind. She'd overtaxed herself, looking after two extra people; her appalling diet of rich foods and fats had finally caught up with her; the stairs had proved too much for her heart. "What in the world is the matter?"

She held out both hands as if she were cradling a tiny baby. Her eyes, when she looked at him, were opaque with fear. "It's Emily, Lucas," she whispered. "Something's happened to her. I think you'd better come."

Monique knew the doctor's her frail old grandmother was trying. "And you can't bear to tell her that until you shook her to watch it," she said, then let a strangely pause...

CHAPTER TEN

GIVEN his grandmother's propensity for exaggeration, Lucas didn't exactly buy her dramatic claim, but that didn't prevent his heart from rioting briefly within his chest cavity.

Controlling the urge to race up the stairs in a panic, he took her by the arm and led her to a chair. "Don't upset yourself, Bea. I'm sure Emily's just fine."

"But she's not!" Bea insisted. "Lucas, she's just lying there in the bed and...bubbling."

"Bubbling?" He smiled at the description. "I don't think I've ever come across that particular condition before. She's becoming more inventive all the time."

But his grandmother wasn't about to be put off and slapped at his hand with rare impatience. "No! Lucas, I'm afraid she's dying! There's a rattling sound every time she breathes and when I spoke to her she didn't seem to know who I was."

A thrill of fear raced up his spine. Only years of practice kept his face reassuringly neutral. "Perhaps I'd better take a look, then."

"Perhaps you had." Monique's voice sliced across the table, rife with censure. "Because if anything happens to my granddaughter, Lucas Flynn, I shall hold you accountable."

"Stay here, both of you. I'll go at once."

He took the stairs three at a time, all the while telling himself that it was just another ruse on Emily's part. Hadn't she paved the way last night for this little scene to take place, complaining vaguely of not feeling well only after she'd partied for hours and seduced him into making love to her?

Yet she'd been well enough to find the skill and energy to reduce him to quivering exhaustion!

Her door stood ajar and he wasn't even at the threshold before he thought he heard it: the impaired gasp of lungs laboring to function as they fought the threat of drowning. Still he didn't want to believe—didn't dare to.

Approaching the bed, he assumed the sort of superior manner that he detested in others of his profession. "Well, Emily, are we not feeling a hundred percent this morning?"

She opened her eyes at the sound of his voice and he was appalled at the blankness he saw there, as if she were staring at a stranger. Or, worse, at nothing.

"Emily," he said again, this time unable to subdue the throb of alarm in his voice. "Can you see me? Do you know who I am?"

"Lucas..." His name seemed to percolate from her throat, making it plain what Bea had meant when she'd used the word "bubbling".

He watched the shallow rise and fall of Emily's chest and cursed inwardly. Hell and damnation, he had enough letters behind his name to qualify him five times over to be a doctor, yet he couldn't lay hands on so much as a stethoscope! Not that he needed anything but the senses he'd been born with both to see and hear that her rate of respiration was clocking in at about forty a minute, rapid enough even for a layman to realize that something was definitely and seriously amiss.

The grandmothers, who naturally enough had ignored his advice and followed him upstairs, hovered in the doorway and he didn't need to look to know that his anxiety had communicated itself to them threefold and that they teetered on the verge of panic. Dear Lord, he didn't need them falling apart now!

"Mrs. Lamartine," he said, making a split-second decision, "there's a phone in my room. I want you to call the hospital right now. Tell them to meet us at the emergency entrance—"

"Wouldn't it be better to ask them to send an ambulance?"

"We can't afford the time," he said bluntly.

She pushed her way past him to see for herself the shape Emily was in. For once, her phenomenal self-possession deserted her and pure dread cracked her voice. "Oh, *mon Dieu!*"

He took her by the shoulders and forcibly turned her away from the bed. "Make that call, Monique. Let them know we'll be there within the half-hour and that we're bringing in a patient showing signs of acute adult pulmonary distress."

He uttered the last four words slowly and distinctly. With a courage he had to admire, she pulled herself together and repeated, "Acute adult pulmonary distress."

"Right. Get on it," he said, and gave her a gentle push toward the door and watched her hobble away before turning his attention to his own grandmother.

"Bea, I need you here. Emily's all tangled up in the sheets and soaked through with perspiration. Sponge her off, get her into a fresh nightgown or robe—whatever you can find—and have her ready to be moved by the time I've brought the car around to the front door."

He was striding away when Emily spoke again, her voice a pale thread of sound drifting weakly after him. "Lucas, don't...leave me...."

"Not a chance," he said, returning briefly to her bedside and stroking the hair out of her eyes. "Not a snowball's chance in hell, sweetheart!"

She lay feather-light against his shoulder as he carried her down the stairs a few minutes later. "Keep her upright as much as possible," he instructed Bea, settling her in the back seat of the station wagon. "It'll help her respiration."

Within five minutes they were on their way, with Monique beside him railing at the slowness of their progress even though he broke all the speed limits. Just as they approached the boundary of April Water, a highway patrol motorcyclist spotted the car and pulled in behind them, lights flashing.

Lucas barely drew to a halt. "Medical emergency," he said tersely, before the helmeted police officer had a chance to open his mouth. "I need an escort to the hospital."

The officer swept an assessing glance over Emily, cradled against Bea's shoulder, and didn't argue. Revving up his motorcycle, he said, "Follow me," and, sirens screaming, cut a path through the thickening traffic in the town, shaving precious minutes off their journey and bringing them to the emergency entrance of April Water General just under the time Lucas had allowed.

The hospital personnel had done their part. Doctors, nurses and lab technicians were there in force, poking and poring over Emily. But the damnable thing was, no one could agree on a diagnosis.

The emergency physician, Martin Jamieson, knew of Lucas through the medical grapevine and called him into a side office. "I didn't want to say anything in front of the elderly relatives," he said, shaking his head, "but this case has us completely baffled."

They'd been messing around with her for over an hour and this was the best they could do? "Damn it, man!" Lucas exploded. "You must have come up with something!"

The other man handed him Emily's chart. "We've run all the usual tests, Dr Flynn: taken her vital signs, checked her blood gases, white blood count—everything you'd do if you were calling the shots."

"She's on oxygen?"

"Yes."

Lucas frowned at the clipboard in his hand and worried his lower lip between his teeth. "Her temperature's elevated. You could be looking at some sort of viral infection, possibly pneumonia. You ordered a chest X-ray?"

Martin Jamieson nodded. "Results just came in. There's fluid on her lungs, no question about it."

"Then you need to get a culture. You can't hazard a guess at medication without one."

"We're trying but she's not very responsive."

Oh, she was responsive enough, given the right circumstances, and Lucas would inspire her now, because he'd be damned if he'd sit idly by and let her just fade away! They had too much to look forward to.

He flipped the chart closed. "Let me try."

Jamieson shrugged and waved him toward the cubicle at the far end of the hall. "Be my guest. We're here when you need us."

Although they had her propped up with pillows, her respiration was still labored, the rattling in her chest as pronounced as when he'd brought her in. "Emily," he said, sliding onto the stool beside her bed and chafing her hand. "You've got to help me."

Her eyes fluttered open briefly, deep brown pansies as soft as velvet. "You came to see me," she breathed, gasping out the words.

"I told you I wouldn't leave you, sweetheart."

She smiled and curled her fingers weakly around his. "I know. I know...everything about you."

Did she? Did she have the faintest inkling of the thoughts racing through his head? Of the dread gnawing at him that left his insides raw with pain? Of the guilt and blame weighing him down until he wanted to die?

"I need your help," he repeated urgently, the fear rising to scald his throat.

"Anything at...all," she murmured, her eyes drifting closed again, "but I think I'll...have a little...sleep first."

"You've got to cough for me, Emily," he said flatly, deciding to save finesse for another day.

"Oh, Lucas," she sighed, "how can you be..." she stopped and fought for another shallow breath "...so unromantic?"

"To hell with romance! There'll be time for that after we've found out what's got your breathing all fouled up." He slid an arm around her shoulder and indicated with a jerk of his head for the nurse waiting outside the cubicle to lend a hand. "Come on, sweet Emily," he said firmly. "We can't do this alone. You've got to do your part."

Afterward, she was so exhausted that she slid into sleep before he'd laid her head back against the pillows. While the nurse hurried the sample to the lab, he pulled the stool closer to the bed and watched with troubled eyes as Emily continued her solitary fight.

Beyond the curtains, the sounds of another day in Emergency filtered around the perimeter of his mind but the focus of his attention never wavered. He knew her rate of respiration exactly without once being aware of counting. His eyes tracked the monitor beside her bed and absorbed the information there without his consciously assessing it.

Halfway through the morning, they came to move her to ICU. The grandmothers, he realized belatedly, were still in the waiting area, fortifying themselves with bad coffee and doughnuts.

"Go out and buy yourselves a decent lunch," he told them, handing over all the money in his wallet. "The last thing I need right now is for the pair of you to OD on hospital food."

"What are you doing for my granddaughter?" Monique asked him, but the snap had gone from her voice and he found himself looking down at a very old, very frightened lady.

"My best, Mrs. Lamartine," he said gently.

"Is your best going to be good enough, Lucas Flynn?"

He closed his eyes because he couldn't face the pleading in hers. "I hope so."

The afternoon dragged by and his best amounted to no more than holding Emily's hand. By sunset her condition had deteriorated to the point that her only option was to be hooked up to a ventilator.

Around him, specialized personnel buzzed with concern and sympathy. But he felt a rage growing within him, a fury so intense that he was ready to split apart from the force of it and knew he had to get out of that room, away from the fear and frustration crowding his mind. He could not see past them, could not function with the clinical objectivity crucial to saving her.

He waited until she fell into another fitful sleep before stealing away. "I'll be downstairs if there's any change," he told her nurse.

He had no idea where exactly, and was astonished when he ended up in the hospital chapel. He wasn't a praying man, never had been. Yet there he was, seeking help in the only place in the entire building that didn't depend on man's high-tech scientific advances to earn its keep.

"All right," he challenged, the rage continuing to grow, "do Your stuff. Prove You're up there and that You give a damn!"

The silence consumed him.

Slumping onto the plain wooden pew, he stared at the candles flickering on the white-cloth-covered table in front of him and realized that the halo around the flames was caused by the tears filming his eyes. Tears of anger, tears of impotence. Because once again someone was dying and once again he was helpless to prevent it.

The difference was, if he failed this time there would be no going on. No marking time, numbed by the dull placebo of professional detachment.

"I have to find myself again," he'd told her, the night she'd forced him to look beyond his chronic self-involvement, when what he should have said was, You've given me back myself, Emily. Through you, I've found a sense of personal commitment to something other than that petri dish you accused me of revering too much. Tomorrow's exciting again, because of you.

But he'd been too proud, too stubborn, too bloody stupid. And now he was being punished. She was life and energy, light and sunshine. She made him want, she made him hope. She was the past he'd lost and the future he'd been afraid he'd never find.

But most of all she was his present, his *now*. It was all anyone had—one of two certainties. And he was losing her to the other—death.

He was a qualified physician and surgeon, with all the skills and knowledge inherent in the titles, and he could do nothing but hold her hand while she slipped away from him. Worse, he was a man who hadn't once found the courage to tell her that he loved her.

To do so now amounted to too little, too late. It would take a miracle to save her and that was God's province, not his. If indeed there was a God....

There was nothing. No clap of thunder, no brilliant shaft of light. Just silence and emptiness and the utter futility of his attempts to heal and save.

The waste was endless, the litany of failure parading through his mind: infants dead before they were born; children deformed by crippling disease and abandoned by parents too weary of the fight to exist to find it worth the effort; youths mutilated by war, their span of time between innocence and maturity marked by missing limbs and vacant eyes. Old people burying grandchildren. Sydney.

The pressure built, crazing the dam of his emotions with tiny fractures. He had never mourned those losses, merely buried them under an objective regret that had left him as arid as the deserts he'd loathed so fiercely.

But this, his last grandiose effort at preserving the sanctity of life, marked a new level of arrogance. He groaned as the memory unrolled. "Dry toast and clear tea. It's been known to work wonders on women suffering from the vapors," he'd sneered disbelievingly, at what could well have been the onset of her illness and the time when it might have been most within his power to halt whatever ravaged her now.

He could not deal with it, could not face his utter culpability.

Sinking his head into his hands, he let the sobs tear loose, awesome in their power, flattening before them all those barriers behind which he'd hidden for so long and leaving him exposed as the bankrupt he really was. Emily would die as she had lived: without any help from him.

"Oh, God...oh, God...!" Laced with agony, the words escaped, not in blasphemy but in supplication for a forgiveness he didn't deserve and for the chance to make reparation before it was too late.

Behind him, the door whispered quietly open. Bea's hand, which had comforted him from the time he'd been born, through all his troubles, great or small, came to rest on his shoulder.

Monique Lamartine stood beside her. He looked up at them, knew they saw the emotional storm that had swept over him, and he didn't care. He had nothing left behind which to hide: no pride, no arrogance, no hope.

"We thought you might be here, Lucas," his grandmother said. "Have you found any answers yet?"

He shook his head. "No."

Bea stroked his face lovingly and it was all he could do not to break down again and bawl like a kid. "Bless you, darling. We're sure you will."

"I wish I shared your confidence." Damn it, his voice trembled like a leaf in a storm. "Gran, I don't know what to do next."

Monique spoke for the first time. "Then you've come to the right place to find out." She leaned on her cane with both hands and looked him squarely in the eye. "I'm counting on you to save my granddaughter, Lucas. You're not going to let me down."

He had done nothing to deserve either her confidence or her trust. That she offered both without condition fired him with a resolve that rose out of the void within him and channeled his grief into sudden, unshakeable determination. "No," he said. "I'm not."

"Is there anything we can do to help?" The light of battle glowed in her eyes.

About to palm her off with the usual "go home and get some rest" advice, he suddenly switched course. "Yes," he said. "I've searched over and over for a clue to what started her illness and come up empty every time. We've lived under the same roof with her for days, eaten the same meals, drunk the same water, yet although we remain healthy she's—" he veered away from the unthinkable "— not. There are no apparent holes in the puzzle yet clearly something, somewhere, is missing. Help me find it."

"How?" Bea looked defeated already, but Monique wasn't so ready to surrender.

"By going over every minute of every day, Beatrice," she said tartly. "Put your mind to work."

"Fill in the blanks for me," Lucas said. "That evening I spent with Tamara Golding's son, for example, did Emily go out, do anything different from the usual? *Think,*" he urged, at the vacant response his question elicited. "Where else might she have been without us, who else might...know...?"

He saw the same answer spring to life in their eyes that occurred to him. "Bruce Anderson!" he exclaimed softly.

"Do you think...?" Bea sounded uncertain.

"Let's get him down here and find out," Monique said.

He showed up within the hour.

"Give me an exact run-down of the times you spent with her," Lucas said, flipping open Emily's file and waiting with pen poised. "The places you went, the things you did, the food you ate, everything."

Anderson's shrug didn't hold out a whole lot of hope. "You already know everything there is to tell. You were there the entire time."

"Not the entire time. What about the first day you met her? She supposedly went for a walk with you that same evening and came back hours later. What took so long?"

He saw the other man's defences go up, heard the resentment in his voice when he replied, "How's that relevant to what's happening now?"

"Damn it, man, answer the question! At this point, we don't know what's relevant and what's not."

"All right." Anderson spun on his heel and commenced pacing back and forth. "We walked along the river bank for about two, maybe three miles. Sat on a bluff and talked a while, strolled back. That's it. All the other times were spent at your grandmother's house except for last night, and you ought to know better than I what took place then."

Lucas flung down the pen and massaged the back of his neck. Had it really been less than twenty-four hours since he'd made love to her? Since she'd shattered in his arms, convulsing around him and sending him spinning out of control?

He looked at Anderson in despair. "And that's all? You haven't missed out anything?"

"Listen, I'm a cop. I'm used to picking up on details. And I don't overlook them because experience has taught me it's the little things that make a difference. So no, I haven't left anything...."

His pacing had grown more agitated as he'd spoken but suddenly it stopped and he froze. "I saw her one other time," he said slowly. "At the beginning of last week—the day she went looking for your cat, Mrs. Lamartine."

"I thought *you* found the cat." Lucas had felt decidedly put out when, apparently not content with the tradition of always getting his man, the Mountie had seen fit to cover himself with more glory by finding Robespierre as well.

"I did. But I found Emily, too, in the garden at Belvoir. She was in that gazebo thing down near the river."

"The belvedere," Monique said. "You remember it, Lucas. It was a favorite place for all of you when you were children."

"What was she doing there?" He tossed the question at Anderson.

"She just said she was looking for her grandmother's cat. I was a bit surprised that she'd even go near the place, actually. It was obviously a rodent haven."

A bell chimed faintly in some deep recess of Lucas's mind, a germ of fragmented knowledge to do with a disease related to....

"Wait a minute," he said, scrambling to hold onto whatever it was that had rippled the surface of his memory before it sank into oblivion. "Run that last bit by me again."

"The place was overrun with rodents. The evidence was everywhere. It didn't bother her, though."

"It wouldn't have," Lucas said slowly. "She was never afraid of things like that. What was she doing when you found her?"

"Nothing." The Mountie shrugged. "Sitting on a bench. Tried to get me to join her—some mouse had paid a visit and she wanted us to meet—but I persuaded her to leave."

"You don't strike me as a man who'd be afraid of mice, Mr. Anderson," Bea remarked.

"I'm not. It was more the whole atmosphere of the place. Full of dust that she'd stirred up, probably from the cushions. They were falling apart, as I recall."

"I dare say." Monique nodded. "It's been several years since anyone bothered with the belvedere."

"That could be it!"

All three started as Lucas slammed his hand on the clipboard.

"Huh?" Anderson muttered.

But explanations would have to wait. Lucas needed to confirm his suspicions, then figure out the next step to take. "You've been feeling OK?" he thought to ask the startled Canadian just before heading out of the door. "No flu-like symptoms, no breathing difficulties?"

The other man shook his head, baffled. "None. Never felt better."

"Good." Lucas lifted his hand in a salute. "Look after the ladies, will you? I've got things to take care of. And whatever you do keep clear of that belvedere. Rope it off and don't let anyone near it."

Emily was still sleeping when he showed up in her room again just before dawn. "Hey," he said softly, drawing the stool up close beside her bed and folding her hand in his, "there's something I forgot to tell you."

The ventilator, one of the older types that looked like a vertical concertina, hissed rhythmically in reply, but she didn't stir. Her lashes remained thick and dark on her cheek and her hand lay unresisting in his.

"We're going to win this one, Emily," he informed her, with a damn sight more conviction than he felt.

He'd told himself more or less the same thing when he'd confronted her team of medical personnel in the conference room located outside the intensive care unit. "I think we're looking at a case of hantavirus pulmonary syndrome," he'd told them, knowing in advance the reaction he'd stir up.

Of them all, only Hal Stafford, director of ICU, had had any inkling of what he was talking about. "That's a very rare viral infection," he'd pointed out. "How long before we'll know for sure?"

"It'll take a while for blood tests to confirm it, but the patient's recent history fits the progression of the disease." He'd swung his attention to the others, adding for their benefit, "It's transmitted to people who inhale the dust of infected animals, specifically deer mice and other rodents."

"And she's been exposed?" The question had been fielded from a nurse on the fringe of the group gathered around him.

"Yes." He'd indicated the research manuals spread out on the table in front of him. "Usually the condition starts with flu-like symptoms which disappear within a day or two then reappear, much more severely, a few days after that."

"And the cure?" All eyes had fixed on him hopefully.

Lucas had sucked in a deep breath and exchanged a telling glance with Stafford. There'd been no point in dissembling. "There is no certain cure. Of those who contract the disease, about fifty percent die. Why the rest survive is anyone's guess."

"So what are you saying?" a junior internist had asked. "That we have to rely on—?"

"Antibiotics, intubation, blind faith. Anyone got any better ideas?" He'd glared at the faces in front of him, willing them to contradict him, to tell him that he'd overlooked a miracle drug, a complicated surgical procedure that would improve her chances of recovery.

He'd met with silence.

"I think that's all I can contribute here," he'd said. "I'll be at Ms. Lamartine's bedside if anyone comes looking for me."

It was as well they hadn't tried to stop him with a lot of nonsense about protocol allowing only physicians with hospital privileges to take charge of patient care, because he'd have dealt very brutally with any sort of interference.

Emily needed him and this was one time he wasn't about to let her down. If she couldn't find the strength to fight, he'd do it for her. Because, come hell or high water, she was going to beat this thing.

"For both our sakes, sweetheart," he said urgently now, leaning close and willing her to hear. "So that we can be together, Emily...you and I and... Oh, damn it!"

He pressed her hand to his mouth, swallowed the grief threatening to erupt inside, and tried again. "Damn it, Emily Jane, you've got to help me fight this thing. I can't do it alone."

The ventilator sighed a response.

That morning, with the sun still little more than a hint of gold on the eastern rim of the sky, formed the pattern for the next four days and nights. Endless hours of watching and waiting. Of eyes so gritty with fatigue that sometimes he couldn't see straight. Of moments of hope strung too briefly between minutes of plummeting despair.

Of coming out of her room and facing her grandmother. Of seeing the old lady's indomitable refusal to bow to defeat and taking strength from it.

"Lucas, darling," Bea entreated regularly. "Come home and rest a while."

But all he would agree to was snatching an hour's sleep in the doctors' lounge, stretched out on a sofa too short for a man of his height. Mostly, though, he catnapped in the chair beside her bed, one eye always watchful for her slightest movement, one ear always alert to her slightest sound.

"This is bloody impossible! Unacceptable!" he'd raged quietly when informed it would take at least two weeks for results to come in on her blood tests. Not that it really made any difference. In the final analysis, her recovery depended on something beyond the scope of medical technology.

"She can't go on like this very much longer," Hal Stafford warned on the fifth day.

Lucas would not, *could not,* accept the idea. "She's held on this long."

"She's losing ground, Lucas."

She was reduced to transparent beauty, the tint of her warm apricot skin paler now, her cheekbones too sharply defined, her lashes sinking a little in the hollows beneath her eyes. But he would not admit that she was losing the battle.

Hal shook his head in silent sympathy and left him alone with her again.

Another night fell, sneaking up without his noticing. He hated the night. It came in like a thief and struck at people when they were at their most vulnerable. Like the time she'd stolen into his room and into his heart.

Why had he denied it for so long and robbed them both of time, the one thing they could never reclaim?

"Forgive me," he begged, holding her hand to his cheek. "Let me make it up to you, my love."

Up, down, up, down. The accordion bellows of the ventilator continued their unchanging rhythm and all at once he couldn't tolerate the noise or the movement any longer. The determination that had driven him this far faltered, his stamina undermined by a fear and emptiness so deep that he doubted he'd ever climb free of them again.

Burying his face in the pillow, he choked, "Don't leave me without letting me tell you that I love you, Emily."

He groped for her hand as he had so many times over the last week. Found it and pressed it to his lips. "Did you hear me?" he whispered. "I said, I love you."

CHAPTER ELEVEN

EMILY had been surrounded by gray, suffocating fog for so long that she'd almost forgotten the feel of sunlight on her face. Had become quite reconciled to the woolly silence, the moist, oppressive atmosphere. But the shadowy figure calling to her spirit, beckoning her toward the dawn, was very persistent. Heavy-limbed, she fought her way through the clinging veils and reached to grasp his beckoning hand.

"I love you," he said, coaxing her toward the light.

She had yearned to hear that voice, those words, for so long that she almost faltered, certain they were another figment of a starving imagination, another dream destined to go unfulfilled.

"Did you hear me?" he said, his voice echoing through the mist. "I love you, Emily."

The light grew brighter, penetrating her closed eyelids and illuminating her lost inner world with soft radiance. She wanted to call out to him, tell him that she heard, that she believed, but her voice was held hostage by some foreign object that filled her throat and left her vocal cords paralysed.

He was close enough now, though, that she could feel him—the warmth of his skin against hers, the energy of his touch. Wait for me, she cried silently, flexing her fingers in entreaty.

He understood. He brought his strong arms around her, and the heat of his body burned away the fog until all that was left were little tendrils of mist draping the most quiet corners of her mind.

"Come back to me, Emily," he ordered her, his voice all husky with a sort of desperate hope. "Open your eyes."

Easy for you to say, she'd have replied if her voice had been working. Didn't he know what a burden eyelids had to bear, raising and lowering lashes like window blinds every time a person blinked?

"Look at me, sweetheart," he said.

Oh, he was a pain, bullying her at every turn!

"Why?" She tried to force the question past the obstruction in her throat and managed only to mangle the word beyond recognition.

"Don't try to talk," he said. "You're on a ventilator."

With a monumental effort, she opened her eyelids a crack. He hovered in front of her, a dark, fuzzy outline haloed in dim light.

His breath sifted over her face. "Do you know me, Emily?"

She blinked again and tried to sharpen her focus. His features swam above her, a little blurry still, but not enough that she didn't recognize the intense blue of his gaze burning away the lingering remains of the fog. Not enough that she couldn't see where exhaustion had painted gaunt shadows under his eyes and left his mouth pinched with anxiety.

She nodded and feasted on the sight of him. How could she not know him? He was her life.

"Hi," he said, holding her hand to his cheek. "Welcome back, angel." But the smile tilting lopsidedly at his mouth was uncertain and, for all that he tried to hide it, his body heaved with sudden, suppressed emotion.

She curled her fingers around the rough texture of his jaw and tried with that simple gesture to still the trembling that shook him so unmercifully. It's all right, she wanted to say. I hadn't gone very far and never doubted that I'd find my way back to you.

But he didn't know that and, turning his face, pressed a kiss to her palm. A tear splashed against her wrist and others clung to his long black lashes.

She thought her heart would break. He had always been so strong, so sure. She had never thought to see him so vulnerable.

She reached out to stroke his hair and, when he would have turned away from her, forced him to look at her.

"Hell," he muttered, swiping at his face with his forearm and trying to pretend he wasn't as subject to human weakness as any other man. "How did this sneak up on me?"

She shook her head, brought his hand to the ventilator and pleaded with her eyes for him to remove the tube from her throat so that she could tell him that she'd never loved him more than she did right at that moment.

He immediately turned professional on her. "I know the ventilator's a nuisance but it saved your life, Emily."

You saved my life, she told him with her eyes.

Either he didn't understand or he chose to ignore her. "It kept you going when your lungs gave out, and you can't just fire it and pick up where you left off simply because you're feeling a bit better. You'll have to be weaned off it, a little at a time." He leaned across the bed and made some sort of adjustment to the machine. "We'll begin slowly, like this. Later on, if you're still doing well, we'll reduce it further."

Then, seeming to realize that he'd allowed himself to be distracted, he went on, "Meanwhile, you're my prisoner and I intend to make the most of it."

He rolled the stool on which he was sitting closer to the bed and trapped her hand—the one not hooked up to all sorts of tubes and plastic bags—between both of his. "Do you know how long you've been lying here in this hospital bed, Emily?"

She shook her head, then felt her eyes fly wide in shock when he told her, "Six days. In a few hours it'll be Saturday morning."

Not possible, she thought. How could she have lost a week of her life?

This time, he read her mind. "I know. It's been a long, hard haul and you've got a way still to go. But you're going to make it, my darling, because I can't live without you."

"My darling," he'd called her! She stared at him, the accelerated thunder of her heart drowning out the hiss and sigh of the ventilator.

"I've run up against a lot of stumbling blocks in the last week," he continued, "and I still don't have all the answers I've been looking for. But one thing I know for sure is that I've been running for years, Emily, because I was too big a fool to know that what I needed, what I really wanted, was right here, with you. Now the running is over."

What about Sydney? Frustrated, she willed him to hear the question and answer it, because how could they simply ignore so large a chunk of his past?

"I've made a lot of mistakes," he said, staring reflectively at the window beyond which the sky showed the faintest hint of blush-pink.

Are you telling me that Sydney was one of them? she demanded silently.

"The devil of it is, I didn't really realize how many mistakes until recently. I thought I'd made the right choices and been cheated." His gaze came back to rest on her face and she saw a peace and acceptance in his expression that were new. "But the fact of the matter is, I cheated myself. Worse, I cheated other people, most of all you."

What about Sydney?

"I don't think Sydney knew," he said, some telepathic part of his brain at last connecting with Emily's. "Mostly, I suppose, because we had so much else in common—professional goals, mainly, which at the time seemed noble enough to erase more personal needs, and friendship. We really liked each other, I won't deny that, but I'm not sure we ever needed each other."

He lifted his shoulders in a self-deprecating shrug. "I'll turn thirty-seven in November, Emily, and I've only just discovered that that's what love is all about: needing and being needed. Not in the sense of loving a person because you need her but needing her because you love her. As I love you."

Her eyes filled with tears of gladness at that, and they rolled down her face unchecked. He misunderstood.

"Have I left it too late, Emily?" he muttered urgently.

She shook her head again and sent the tears spinning in great sparkling arcs. She drew his hand to the spot just beneath her breast where her heart thumped with joy and held it there, telling him the only way she knew how that it was his for the rest of time.

He understood.

They'd been married nearly five months when the new medical research wing of the April Water General Hospital was formally opened, just before Christmas that year. As head of the facility, Lucas had been involved in the project from the start and had quickly established so fine a reputation that people in town seemed to think he was the best thing to happen since the invention of penicillin.

But he wasn't as smart as they all liked to believe, because he'd completely misdiagnosed the subtle changes taking place with his wife. Not because the bloom had worn off the marriage and he'd begun to take her for granted, however. Anything but! He'd plied her with care, worrying that the after-effects of her illness would leave a permanent mark on her health and relaxing only when, as winter advanced, she'd added a few more pounds to those she'd regained during her recovery.

She should have expected that his protective instincts would switch to red alert when she arrived home late from a last-minute shopping trip in San Francisco two days before Christmas.

"You're overdoing things," he scolded, glaring at her across the table in the dining room at Belvoir. "You've worked non-stop in the last few months, what with selling one business and starting another, then arranging the wedding and getting this house back into shape, not to mention moving Monique and Consuela in with Bea over at Roscommon and finding a housekeeper to take over the bulk of the work for them."

"Rubbish!" Fairly bursting with her secret, she tossed aside her serviette and sashayed toward the kitchen to haul the baked chicken tarragon out of the oven. "I thrive on challenge, my darling husband, as you should know. I roped you into marriage, after all, even if it did take me the better part of twelve years."

As she passed by his chair, he reached out one long arm and snagged her around the waist. "Funny," he murmured, sliding a possessive hand under the hem of her dress and up her thigh. "I thought I was the one who proposed."

"Only because I let you think that," she said, melting under his ministrations. "If you haven't yet figured out what a clever, sneaky individual I can be when the occasion justifies it, you've got a lot to learn about women."

"Teach me," he purred, swinging her around so that she sat straddled across his lap.

"Here?"

He nuzzled her neck. "Why not? We've made love just about everywhere else. The kitchen, the bathroom, the living-room floor, the butler's pantry."

"The verandah," she said, her breath tripping in her throat as he trespassed beyond the bounds of dining decency and slipped his thumb inside the leg of her panties.

"The verandah," he agreed, his laughter rumbling against her breasts.

That had been the day just one week before the wedding when Tamara Golding had dropped by unexpectedly for a tour of Belvoir in its restored splendor.

Tamara had never quite forgiven Emily for stealing Lucas from under her nose but any notion she'd had that perhaps he'd decide he'd made the wrong choice had evaporated at the sight of him rearranging his fiancée's clothes as cool as you please and saying, "Great timing, Tamara. Call before you stop by next time, OK?"

She hadn't bothered them again. Instead, she'd sent them a silver wine cooler as a wedding present and turned her energies elsewhere. The last time they'd run into her she'd been on the arm of the most successful realtor in town.

Bruce, on the other hand, kept in touch regularly. They'd received a Christmas card from him just the week before in which he'd mentioned at length the advent of a new love interest in his life.

"Lucas," Emily sighed now, trying hard to behave like the respectable married matron she was supposed to be. The long ivory velvet drapes remained undrawn, after all, and, although the only lights in the room came from the Christmas tree in the front hall and the candles on the table, anyone looking in the window would see at once what that wonderful Dr. Flynn and his wife were up to. "We really must...."

"Yes," Lucas said hoarsely. "We really must, my love. Right here, right now."

She'd thought she'd tell him tomorrow night, Christmas Eve, after dinner was over, when she was curled up against him on the couch in the living room, with the flames dancing in the fireplace and the scent of cedar and pine in the air.

"I did more than shop yesterday," she'd planned to say. "I went to see a specialist first. Pulled rank by telling him who my husband was, and persuaded him to take one more appointment before he flew to Mexico for the holidays."

"Specialist?" he'd say, and she'd regret just a little that she'd had to cause him a moment of anxiety before giving him her most special Christmas gift, one she couldn't wrap in gold foil and scarlet ribbons.

But he was beguiling her with his loving now, with the salad plates still on the table and the wine in his glass barely touched. He was pushing aside the Lamartine sterling with one hand and doing exquisitely wicked things to her with the other, bringing her such pleasure that she couldn't bear not to share every last part of herself with him.

"Lucas," she whispered, feeling him hot and urgent against her, "we're going to have a baby."

To say that she took the wind out of his sails was putting it mildly. "You're *what?*" he said, rearing back as if a viper had sprung from her ripely pregnant breasts.

"Having a baby," she said again, and when that didn't seem to register added, "It must have happened one time when we—"

"I know how babies are made," he said in a stunned voice. "But you said you couldn't—that when you were married to what's-his-name you hadn't...."

She shrugged. "I was wrong. Or else I simply waited for the right man to be the father."

Propping her on the edge of the table, he regarded her wonderingly. "A baby," he said, still in the same, star-struck tone. "Are you sure?"

"I saw a specialist this morning, in San Francisco."

His gaze sharpened with concern. "Why? Is there something wrong, something—?"

"No." She smiled and leaned down to kiss him, wishing he'd stop asking her questions and pick up where he'd left off before she'd blurted out the news. "I'm perfectly healthy and progressing exactly as a woman in her eleventh week should."

"Eleventh week!" he exploded. "Specialist! Where the hell do you get off, Emily Jane, keeping secrets like this? Going to some stranger for medical confirmation when you're married to me? Aren't I good enough? Do you think I don't know what to look for? That supervising a pregnancy is beyond my capabilities?"

"Oh, Lucas!" she laughed, stroking his beloved, beautiful face. "I know exactly what you're capable of. You've become my best friend, my lover, my husband, and now you're the father of my baby. You've made me happier than I ever thought it possible to be and given me everything I ever wanted. What I need to hear you tell me now is not how wickedly secretive I've been but that you're happy with the news. That you don't feel you're too old and feeble to take on a child—"

"Woman," he muttered, hoisting her into his arms and making his way up the stairs to their bedroom, "you're pushing your luck!"

"It's just wifely concern," she said, twining her arms around his neck as he deposited her on the bed and pulling him down after her. "I don't want you worn out before your time. You promised me at least forty years of married bliss and I'm planning to hold you to it. I want," she said, gasping a little at the forays he was making over her naked flesh as he stripped away her clothes, "us to sit beside each other on the verandah in our rocking chairs, placid and content as we watch our grandchildren playing, the way our grandparents were when we were young."

"We're a long way from that, Emily," he said, a little short of breath himself as she undid the buttons on his shirt and explored the hard, flat plane of his stomach. "Right now I'm feeling anything but placid—or flaccid!"

"How do you feel, Lucas?" she whispered, yielding to the urgent nudging of his flesh against hers.

"As if I hold the whole world in my arms," he said, sinking into her. "As if I've made a journey through hell and come through it to find heaven on the other side. I love you, Emily Flynn...."

HARLEQUIN PRESENTS®

Everyone has special occasions in their life—an engagement, a wedding, an anniversary...or maybe the birth of a baby.

These are times of celebration and excitement, and we're delighted to bring you a special new series called...

One special occasion—that changes your life forever!

Celebrate *The Big Event!* with great books by some of your favorite authors:

September 1998—BRIDE FOR A YEAR
by Kathryn Ross (#1981)

October 1998—MARRIAGE MAKE UP
by Penny Jordan (#1983)

November 1998—RUNAWAY FIANCÉE
by Sally Wentworth (#1992)

December 1998—BABY INCLUDED!
by Mary Lyons (#1997)

Look in the back pages of any *Big Event* book to find out how to receive a set of sparkling wineglasses.

Available wherever Harlequin books are sold.

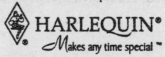

HARLEQUIN®
Makes any time special ™

Take 2 bestselling love stories FREE

Plus get a FREE surprise gift!

Special Limited-Time Offer

Mail to Harlequin Reader Service®

3010 Walden Avenue
P.O. Box 1867
Buffalo, N.Y. 14240-1867

YES! Please send me 2 free Harlequin Presents® novels and my free surprise gift. Then send me 6 brand-new novels every month, which I will receive months before they appear in bookstores. Bill me at the low price of $3.12 each plus 25¢ delivery and applicable sales tax, if any*. That's the complete price, and a saving of over 10% off the cover prices—quite a bargain! I understand that accepting the books and gift places me under no obligation ever to buy any books. I can always return a shipment and cancel at any time. Even if I never buy another book from Harlequin, the 2 free books and the surprise gift are mine to keep forever.

106 HEN CH69

Name	(PLEASE PRINT)	
Address	Apt. No.	
City	State	Zip

This offer is limited to one order per household and not valid to present Harlequin Presents® subscribers. *Terms and prices are subject to change without notice. Sales tax applicable in N.Y.

UPRES-98

©1990 Harlequin Enterprises Limited

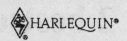 **HARLEQUIN®**

Not The Same Old Story!

 **PRESENTS®**

Exciting, glamorous romance stories that take readers around the world.

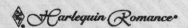 *Harlequin Romance®*

Sparkling, fresh and tender love stories that bring you pure romance.

 HARLEQUIN® *Temptation.*

Bold and adventurous—Temptation is strong women, bad boys, great sex!

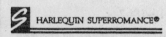 **HARLEQUIN SUPERROMANCE®**

Provocative and realistic stories that celebrate life and love.

 **HARLEQUIN® AMERICAN ROMANCE®**

Contemporary fairy tales—where anything is possible and where dreams come true.

 **HARLEQUIN® INTRIGUE®**

Heart-stopping, suspenseful adventures that combine the best of romance and mystery.

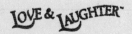 **LOVE & LAUGHTER™**

Humorous and romantic stories that capture the lighter side of love.